PRAISE F

Here are some of the over 100,000 five star reviews left for the Dead Cold Mystery series.

"Rex Stout and Michael Connelly have spawned a protege."

AMAZON REVIEW

"So begins one damned fine read."

AMAZON REVIEW

"Mystery that's more brain than brawn."

AMAZON REVIEW

"I read so many of this genre...and ever so often I strike gold!"

AMAZON REVIEW

"This book is filled with action, intrigue, espionage, and everything else lovers of a good thriller want."

AMAZON REVIEW

GARDEN OF THE DAMNED

A DEAD COLD MYSTERY

BLAKE BANNER

RIGHTHOUSE

ISBN-13: 978-1-63696-003-6

ISBN-10: 1-63696-003-0

Cover design by: Damonza

Printed in the United States of America

www.righthouse.com

www.instagram.com/righthousebooks

www.facebook.com/righthousebooks

twitter.com/righthousebooks

DEAD COLD MYSTERY SERIES

ONE

For reasons I couldn't really put my finger on, it was somehow appropriate. Out the window, April was coaxing the first tender green leaves from bare branches and withered twigs after a dark, cold winter. This seemed like a suitable counterpoint. I tossed the file onto the desk, narrowly missing my feet, and said, "This one looks interesting."

Dehan picked it up, leafed through it, and read the abstract on page one.

"John Doe." She smiled at me in a way that said she wasn't really smiling at me. "Good start." She carried on, "Aged about thirty, found in a dumpster at the corner of Lafayette and Bryant, in the Bronx. No papers, no ID. Clothes suggest a vagrant. Cause of death, a single gunshot wound to the back of the head, possibly a .38. No slug recovered and no blood found in the vicinity." She looked at me. "What makes this interesting?"

I frowned at her and spoke with some severity. "The fact that a young man got murdered."

She raised an eyebrow at me. "No. That is why we should investigate it. That doesn't make it interesting. So far it looks like a guy nobody cares about got whacked by another guy nobody cares about. You said it was interesting, why?"

"Look at the photographs."

She leafed through till she came to the photographs, three six-by-eights. She spread them on the desk and spent a couple of minutes staring at them. They showed a man of about thirty, in old, filthy clothes, lying facedown in a dumpster full of rubble and builder's trash. She shook her head. "Help me out. I'm not seeing it."

I gave a small smirk as I handed her my magnifying glass. "Have a look at his hands."

She stared at the glass a moment and then at me before taking it, then she looked at John Doe's hands. She sat back. "Okay, they appear to be manicured. You are observant, Sensei."

"And the hair. That is definitely a hundred-dollar haircut."

She leaned forward again and studied the photographs. She nodded. "So," she said and handed back the glass. "How do we figure this? He's in the neighborhood of Lafayette, maybe looking for a whore, he gets mugged . . ."

Even as she was saying it, she was seeing the flaws. I said, "Let's suppose he had a thousand-dollar suit that, by some fluke, happened to be the right size for our killer. So he kills him, takes his suit, his shoes, and his watch, plus his wallet. Why then go to the trouble of dressing him as a homeless person and dumping him in a dumpster?"

She looked back at the file.

"Single gunshot wound to the back of the head. Execution style." She shrugged. "These days any kid who wants to be in a gang is likely to shoot you in the back of the head just so he can boast he killed you 'execution style.'"

"True enough." I stood. "But if you look at the ME's report . . ." She leafed through to the report and read while I spoke. "You'll see that entry was at the base of the skull, and the exit wound was where the two clavicles meet above the sternum. Which means the shot was at about a ten- to twenty-degree angle. Like so." I demonstrated. "John Doe was kneeling, the killer was standing behind him."

"Execution style."

I nodded. "You haven't got a lot of dark back alleys around there. It's all mainly big, broad streets and open spaces. Plus we know they searched the area and found no blood, no slug. There was no bleeding inside the dumpster."

Dehan was watching me and nodding. "So it's clear he was killed somewhere else and then thrown in the dumpster."

"Right, so the killer gets him on his knees. Shoots him in the back of the head. He has either already made him strip, or he now strips off his clothes, and he dresses him as a vagrant. Then, presumably in the small hours of the morning, he takes him and dumps him. What benefit does the killer get from doing that?"

Dehan arched her eyebrows and spread her hands. "The benefit he actually got was that the case went cold almost immediately, and if you hadn't pissed off Captain Jennifer Cuevas it would probably have stayed cold."

"Hidden in plain sight." I nodded. "A guy nobody cares about murdered by another guy nobody cares about. So there is probably a missing persons report that relates to this guy, but nobody ever made the connection with our victim, because they assumed he was a vagrant. Let's find out who he is."

"Something else." She tapped the photographs. "Why that particular dumpster? Is it because it was close? Did they own it and they were planning a more thorough disposal, but it went wrong? Maybe it was just random, but I think it's worth looking into."

"Good, I agree."

The next couple of hours were drudgery fuelled by coffee. The dumpster belonged to a company called Hagan's Dumpsters, which was a spawn from a parent company called Hagan Construction, which in turn belonged to Conor Hagan, a guy known to be the head of a clan in the Irish Mob. Hagan's head office was on East 116th Street, one block from the Supreme Criminal Court. You've got to love the Irish and their sense of humor.

I was about to tell Dehan when she stretched out in her chair and sighed. "A lot of people went missing in New York in 2005. But when you filter out the women, guys over thirty-five and under twenty-seven, and people with a criminal record, you wind up with two, and one of them was a car mechanic."

I could hear the printer churning out a photograph. She stood and walked away, coming back a few seconds later with a photograph and a sheet of printed paper. She dropped the photograph in front of me and sat. This was our guy. She read from the printed sheet.

"Sean O'Conor, thirty years old at the time of his disappearance, an attorney specializing in human rights, junior partner at Stanley and Cohen, in Brooklyn. Also worked on a pro bono basis at the Drop-In Center, on Sheridan Avenue, a free representation unit funded by charities, which he helped to set up. There was him, David Foster, and Arnav Singh. The office closed down shortly after Sean disappeared.

"Parents, James and Kathleen O'Conor, apparently still living."

I sat back and scratched my chin.

"So, we have a case of an Irish human rights attorney from Brooklyn found, dressed as a vagrant, murdered execution style, in the Bronx, in a dumpster owned by the Irish Mob."

"Really?"

"Hagan Construction." I told her what I'd found.

"Where do you want to start?"

I stared at Dehan's face. It was a nice thing to stare at, and she stared back at me. It was a thing we did. Other people found it unsettling but it helped us to think.

"My gut," I said, "tells me whatever Sean O'Conor was doing in Brooklyn did not get him killed in the Bronx. I want to talk to his partners at the Drop-In Center, then maybe we have a chat with his mom and dad."

"My thoughts exactly, Sensei. You want to forage some food while I find out where Foster and Singh are?"

I left her to it and made for the deli on the corner.

TWO

I GOT TWO BEEF ON RYE AND DEHAN MET ME OUTSIDE the station, sitting on the hood of my Jaguar. Not many women can sit on the hood of a 1964 Mark II and look good. Mostly you want to move them off so you can get a good look at the car, but Dehan looked like she belonged there. I handed her her sandwich and she began to unwrap it.

"David's office is in Manhattan, but he's at home today. Harbor Road, Oyster Bay, Long Island. I called and they are expecting us."

I opened the car. "I guess we can assume he isn't doing pro bono work anymore."

"Seems a safe bet."

We took the Bronx–Whitestone Bridge and then, at Cunningham Park, we turned east onto the Long Island Expressway and followed that as far as Jericho. The Jericho Oyster Bay Road was long and straight and leafy in the dappled sunshine, and there were cute houses hiding among the trees, with chimney pots poking out and leaded bow windows. It was like driving into a chocolate box.

We arrived at Oyster Bay and crawled through a sleepy town where it seemed almost everybody lived in a mansion, and the small houses were the ones with only five bedrooms and no tennis court. It was a tasteful place, but none had the gaudy ostentatiousness of Manhattan. You had the impression that poverty was not allowed here, not because it was immoral, but because it was in bad taste, like stretched limos and tiepins.

As we turned into Harbor Road, Dehan was looking around her with a kind of rueful air. "Jeez, I bet even the muggers here wear Ralph Lauren and say please and thank you."

"We have become cynics, Dehan. We devote our lives to fighting crime, but have you ever thought what it would be like if we won?"

She didn't answer for a moment, staring out at the rows of sweeping lawns, white picket fences, and rambling houses. "It never crossed my mind," she said at last, "that we might win."

He had an ample driveway, so I pulled in and parked beside his Porsche. As I climbed out and Dehan walked toward the front door, I glanced at the two cars. I thought mine fit better than his. It was less gaudy. Maybe I needed a house to go with my car.

David Foster had a polite Latin-American housemaid who opened the door to us. We told her who we were, and she led us out to the pool. It was not warm enough to swim yet, but it was pleasant enough for tasteful pre-prandial drinks on the patio. David was sitting at a white wrought iron table reading some documents, with what looked like a bone-dry martini by his elbow.

He looked up as we approached, smiled agreeably, and stood to greet us. We showed him our badges.

"I am Detective John Stone; this is my partner, Detective Carmen Dehan."

We shook and he gestured toward the table. "Please, take a seat. Can I offer you a drink? You are on duty, so perhaps some homemade lemonade?" He didn't wait for an answer, but turned and said, "Rosalía, *dos vasos de limonada, por favor.*"

She gave a cute little bow and walked back toward the house. We all sat. He was handsome in an Anglo-Saxon sort of way, with sandy hair and blue eyes. He smiled at Dehan and said, "When you called, you mentioned that you wanted to discuss Sean O'Conor with me. I haven't seen Sean for about twelve years. I am not sure what I can tell you about him, but may I ask what your interest is?"

Dehan glanced at me.

I said, "You worked together at the Drop-In Center, on Sheridan Avenue in the Bronx, is that right?"

He smiled. "Yes, there were three of us. They were good times. There was me, Sean, and Arnav . . . Arnav Singh!" He said it as though remembering their names was an achievement of some sort.

Dehan gestured around her. "It seems a long way from this."

"Oh, it is! But my uncle insisted on it. If I was going into his firm, he wanted me to experience life, and the law, at the sharp end. I'm glad I did it, and I'm glad it's over. But your interest is in Sean, not me, I gather. And I am still not sure why."

I asked him, "Do you recall what cases Sean was involved in back then?"

He frowned. "Only vaguely, and I am not sure I would be allowed to discuss them with you. If he discussed them with me in a legal capacity . . ."

"Privilege would extend to you, I understand that. The thing is, Mr. Foster, Sean was murdered, and we believe it may have had something to do with a case he was working on at that time."

His frown had become incredulous. "Murdered? Sean? But that's . . . grotesque! Poor Sean. What on Earth happened?"

Dehan said, "That is what we are trying to find out. I'm not a lawyer, Mr. Foster, but if he was murdered, surely you could be a little flexible."

He nodded. "Of course." He stared hard at the tabletop for a while. "Sean was a bit stereotypic, you know, very much the Irish firebrand. Always ready—a bit too ready if you ask me—to take on the big boys and strike a blow for the underdog." He looked at me and frowned. "That was what always surprised me. One day he just didn't turn up at the Center. Arnav and I stuck it out to the end of the month, but the driving force behind that place had always been Sean. So we just closed up shop and went our separate ways."

"Can you remember any particular cases he was working on just before he disappeared?"

He stared at me. "Is that why he disappeared? Because he was murdered? Twelve years ago?"

I nodded.

"Jesus . . . !" He sighed. "Yeah, his big thing at the time was a squatters' rights case. You should talk to Singh. He and Sean were thick as thieves. He was going up against a big construction company that wanted to evict, or was in the process of evicting, a bunch of people who were squatting in a building. The company wanted to knock down the site and develop it. Of course there were millions—tens of millions—of dollars at stake, but Sean's point was, quite correctly, that the rights of the people who were living there were being trampled on."

Dehan asked, "Can you remember the name of the construction company?"

He shook his head. "I can't, but I do remember him making a big thing at the time of the fact that they were Irish, like him. The whole Irish, Catholic thing was a big deal for him."

Rosalía came out with two glasses and a pitcher of iced lemonade. She poured us a glass each, left the pitcher, and went back inside.

I sipped and Dehan said, "You mentioned he was close to Arnav. You guys stay in touch?"

"No, he moved down to Washington. His thing was playing politics, not my scene. I get more than enough of that at work. But he was smart and ambitious, so he shouldn't prove hard to find. Then there was his church. Not Arnav, Sean."

I frowned at him. "His church?"

"Oh, yes! When I say to you that everything, and I mean everything, revolved around God, Jesus, and the Roman Catholic

Church, I am not exaggerating even a little. I don't know when he found time for his actual, real job, but he used to spend every spare moment he had at the church, doing everything from distributing clothes to running a soup kitchen, reading to little old ladies . . . you name it."

"Some guy." It was Dehan; she was looking skeptical.

"No, don't smirk, Detective. He was the real deal, an honest-to-goodness good guy. I try, let's face it, most of us try and do the best we can. We all care a bit, right? Not him. He was the genuine article. He really cared, completely. If you talk to the priest there, I am sure he will remember him."

I asked him, "What church?"

"St. Mary's, it was . . . let me see if I can remember . . . Lafayette. It was a big church. Old. You know, the ones that actually look like churches. You won't have any trouble finding it. The padre was Irish too. One of those 'O' names."

Dehan said, "O'Neil?"

He snapped his fingers and smiled. "That's the fellow. Father O'Neil, Padraig O'Neil!"

She nodded. "I know it."

Foster had got into his stride. "It's coming back to me now. He had a girl too. You should talk to her, although oddly enough she wasn't Irish. I think she was Venezuelan or Mexican maybe. Anyway, for sure she was Latin American. He was pretty sweet on her. I definitely remember that."

I asked, "Can you remember her name?"

He shook his head. "As I say, he and I weren't real good pals. I think I was too much of a WASP for his taste, Boston Brahmins, English ancestors . . . not his cup of tea. He was a nice guy, though."

We chatted a bit longer, finished our lemonade, and left.

Dehan closed her door and I sat drumming my fingers on the steering wheel. Dehan glanced at me. "Don't tell me, it's too easy."

I grimaced, turned the key in the ignition, and took off.

THREE

JAMES AND KATHLEEN O'CONOR HAD A HOUSE IN Corona, just by the Flushing Meadows Park. It was a nice, detached place on 46th Avenue, which would probably have fit comfortably into David Foster's kitchen. As I pulled up in front of their gate, I paused a moment to think about relative values. I get deep like that sometimes. Dehan said, "You think the pool and the tennis courts are in back?"

I climbed out and looked at her across the roof of the car. The first green leaves of spring were coming out on the plane tree behind her. "Is that the whiff of sour grapes I detect in your voice, Dehan?"

She shook her head. "No, I'm just wondering, what didn't these guys do, that David Foster did do . . . ?"

"If your point is that life isn't fair, you're a little late. We already knew that."

She sighed. "I know."

I pushed through the gate and rang on the bell.

The door opened, and I looked down at a small woman of maybe five feet. She had a squint and short hair, jeans, a pink cardigan, and a mischievous smile.

"Can I help you?"

I showed her my badge. "Detectives Stone and Dehan, NYPD. Are you Kathleen O'Conor?"

"I am, what have I done now?" she said, and grinned.

I smiled back. "Nothing we know of, Mrs. O'Conor. We would just like a quick word with you and your husband, Jim. Is he in?"

"He's watching the TV, for a change. Come in." She walked ahead of us into the front room, speaking as she went. "Jim! Would you turn the feckin' TV off for five minutes? We have visitors."

We followed her in. There was an immensely tall man, with a shock of snow-white hair swept back from his face, folded into an armchair opposite the TV. He fumbled with the remote control, switched off the television, and levered himself to his feet. Once he had managed all that, he smiled. He must have been six foot six if he was an inch.

I told him who we were and they both told us to sit down. I watched Jim lever himself back into his chair, and Kathleen sat on the sofa, next to Dehan, with her feet barely touching the floor.

I sighed. "We need to talk to you about your son, Sean." I pulled the photograph Dehan had printed from my pocket and showed it to them. "Is this Sean O'Conor, your son?"

All the humor drained from their faces. Kathleen put her hand to her mouth and tears glistened in her eyes. Jim seemed to turn gray.

"Yeah. That's our son. Did you find him?"

"I'm afraid I have very bad news. Sean was found murdered."

Kathleen gave a scream. Her eyes went wide and she stared at me. Jim seemed to crumble. He sank back in his chair and put one massive hand over his eyes. Kathleen kept saying, "No! Oh, no! God no, please."

Jim spoke without opening his eyes. "When did this happen? Where has he been all this time? What has he got himself mixed up in . . . ?"

I took a deep breath, but it was Dehan who answered. "It

happened twelve years ago, Mr. O'Conor, but we were only able to identify the body this morning."

Kathleen's hands dropped into her lap. "What?"

Jim opened his eyes. "Twelve feckin' years?"

"Why were we not notified? Why was he not . . ."

"Twelve feckin' years!" Jim said it again, looking around the room as though he might find an explanation on the walls somewhere.

"I know it is hard to understand." Even as I said it, it sounded lame. "We were pretty surprised ourselves. But all his papers had been removed, and he had been dressed in the clothes of a vagrant. There was no possible clue to his identity."

Kathleen's face twisted and she started to sob. "Oh, God bless him, poor Sean!" Dehan put her arm around her.

Jim shook his head. His voice was a rasp. "Who would do a thing like that to my son?"

"That's what we mean to find out."

Dehan said, "We know this is really hard, but if you can help us, if you can answer a few questions for us . . ."

"We can come back later if . . ."

But they were both shaking their heads. Kathleen spoke into her handkerchief, twisting her nose. "I knew it. I knew he was dead. I said so, didn't I, Jim?"

"Ah, sure, we both knew, Kath. It's just, when you come face-to-face with it like that . . ."

"When you have it confirmed. And murdered . . . sweet mother of God, murdered . . ." She started sobbing again.

"Shall I make a cup of tea?" It was Dehan, stroking her back.

Kathleen gripped her hand and looked up into her face. "Would you, love?"

Dehan went out to the kitchen. I heard the cupboard doors bang and the tap hiss.

I said, "Did he ever talk much about his work with you?"

"All the feckin' time!" It was Kathleen, talking into her handkerchief again. She blew her nose. "It's all he ever feckin' talked about. His work, and the f . . . and the church."

Jim said, "He was very devoted to his work, and to the church, Detective."

"Do you recall what he was working on just before he disappeared?"

Jim nodded. "Oh, yes. How could I not? We both do, don't we, Kath?"

"Some feckin' squatters. Lazy feckin' no-good layabouts, want every feckin' thing handed them on a feckin' plate . . ."

She dissolved into tears. Jim watched her a moment, then turned to me. "They had taken over a building on Tiffany Street, in the Bronx. Big, five-story apartment block, so it was. Semi-derelict, no water, no electric, but there must have been some handy lads there 'cause didn't they get it all working? Illegal, like, but still . . ."

"And charge it to the feckin' honest taxpayer!"

"Not at all, Kath! Taxpayers had nothing to do with it."

"So you say!"

I coughed. "So, what did your son have to do with these squatters?"

"Didn't the landlord want to sell the site, so they could tear it down and make offices there? See, it was worth a hell of a lot more as offices than as apartments. So, one of the parishioners at St. Mary's, some down-and-out, one of them squatters, tells Sean they're being evicted, and doesn't he only go and start a case against the company that's selling the site. He claims agents for the company had taken rent from the residents, and therefore owed them compensation for evicting them."

"Can you remember the name of the company?"

He gave a dry laugh. "Well, that was another thing. It turns out, according to Sean, the company selling the property and the company buying the property are both owned by the same parent company, and they both have city officials sitting on the board of directors. It stank to high hell. And he was goin' after them, goin' for the jugular, so he was."

"Can you remember the name?"

"Remember it? I'll never feckin' forget it. Hagan Construction. That was the parent company, belonged to Conor Hagan, and you being a policeman, you'll be familiar with the name. Any Irishman who has lived in the Bronx is familiar with that name. Head of the Hagan clan, a big shot in the Irish Mob, a very dangerous man to cross." His bottom lip curled and he began to sob. "I never wished so bad that I'd had a coward for a son. May God forgive me, wasn't it his courage and his faith that cost him his life?"

Dehan came in with a tray, four cups, and a pot of tea. She set it down on the coffee table and started to pour. While she did, I sat back and stared out their bow window at the tree across the road.

Dehan handed me a cup and sat down next to Kathleen. I said, "So Sean was taking a case on behalf of the residents of this building on Tiffany Street, against Conor Hagan."

"Residents?" It was Kathleen. "Squatters and parasites, more like!"

A flash of irritation crossed Jim's face. "He was a good Christian, Kath. He lived by his faith . . ."

"And feckin' died for it!"

Dehan cut in before it escalated. "I believe he was active at a church in the Bronx."

Jim sipped. "St. Mary's. He was born in the Bronx, and we moved out here when he was a young lad, to get away from the crime. But we stayed in contact with the priest, a good man so he was, always ready to help, if he could."

"Father O'Neil. So Sean must have had friends at the church."

"Oh, he did that."

Kathleen smiled briefly. "And a lovely girl. God alone knows what she thought when he just vanished. Mexican, but a lovely, sweet child, as devout as he was. Isn't that how they met? In the soup kitchen, and delivering clothes during the bitter winter. They were both besotted, bless them."

Dehan asked, "What was her name, Kathleen?"

"God forgive me, I can't remember. Isn't it a shame? I only met her the one time when he brought her over for dinner. But it's that long ago, I cannot remember her name. Can you remember, Jim?"

He shook his head. "No. It was one of them Mexican, Spanish names. Maria, was it? Or Carmen . . . ? I don't recall."

I asked, "Any idea how we could find her or contact her?"

Kathleen looked at me as though I were a bit slow. "Sure, won't he have her address and telephone number upstairs?"

I smiled. "Upstairs?"

"Of course! I have all his stuff upstairs. His computer, all his papers, his diary . . . everything. I mean, until today . . ." Her face started to fold up into wet grief again. "We had no idea if he was coming back. He might have turned up at any time, walked through the door . . . !"

I watched her a moment, trying to conceive what kind of hell she must be going through. I couldn't even begin. I turned to Jim. I saw the same hell behind his eyes, but I knew from his face he was going to keep it together until we were gone, until Kathleen couldn't see him.

I said, "We need to take his things away and examine them. Have you any objection? It will all be returned to you after the investigation."

"We have no objection. Take what you need. Just catch the bastard who did this to our son."

I pulled out my phone and called the 43rd. "I need a CSI team to collect evidence from the following address . . ." I told her where it was. Then added, "It is just papers and IT stuff. No, no body."

When I hung up, Kathleen said, "Of course, it all depends how much was taken in the burglary."

Dehan sat back and sighed. I tried not to look at her. "Burglary?"

"Didn't it all happen at the same feckin' time. They say it never rains but it pours. The very night after he never came home, didn't we have a feckin' break-in? They went into his room, God alone knows what they expected to find up there . . ."

Jim shrugged. "The policeman said it was probably opportunistic, you know, broke in on the off chance."

I stared at them both for a moment, trying to fathom the depths of human stupidity.

"It didn't occur to you, or the cop, that his disappearance and the break-in might be connected?"

They looked blank. Kathleen said, "No. Why would it?"

I smiled. "Sure, why would it? Did anything go missing from Sean's room?"

"I couldn't tell you," said Jim. "He kept all his stuff very private. Nobody was allowed to touch it, but I wouldn't have thought so. Sure, they left the computer, didn't they? A real fancy one at that, and who'd be interested in a lot of papers? So you're probably all right."

I nodded and looked at Dehan. "No doubt." I made to stand. "We won't take up any more of your time. A van will be here shortly to bag up and take the stuff from Sean's room. Please don't go in there or disturb anything. We'll keep you posted as to any developments."

We left them holding each other at the door and climbed into the Jag. Dehan frowned at me. "You don't want to look through his stuff before we leave?"

I shook my head. "I'm more interested in what isn't on the computer. We'll go over everything at our leisure back at the station, but I think we'll find anything of interest has already been taken." I fired up the engine. "Where to now, Dehan?"

She smiled. "Sure, isn't it time you spoke to Father O'Neil?"

I nodded. "It sure is."

FOUR

We took the I-678, crossed back over the Bronx–Whitestone Bridge, and arrived at Lafayette Avenue, in Hunts Point, about twenty minutes later. The sun was slipping in the east and evening was insinuating itself into the air. I parked, climbed out of the car, and stood staring at the massive stone temple. I was tired and in need of a beer, but I wanted to talk to Father O'Neil before Dehan and I chewed the cud over a drink.

The church was big, set back from the road in its own grounds and surrounded by trees that made it hard to distinguish the details of the building. The walls were gray stone and the roofs were sharp, red-tiled gables. They looked stark and unhappy against the fragile, early spring sky. The whole thing occupied half a block and was surrounded by a black iron railing, maybe seven feet high.

Dehan pointed at the corner. "The entrance is on Faile Street."

"Let's take a look around before we go in."

I walked east, toward the corner with Bryant. The church railing ended where it joined with the wall of a six-story brownstone apartment block. I stopped outside the door and pointed at the curb. "That's where the dumpster was." I looked back at the church grounds. "What is that, thirty feet from the railing?" I looked at the apartment block. It had a fire escape on either side of the building, with a CCTV camera over the arched doorway. "I'm figuring they didn't bring it down the fire escape. This is a busy street, patrol cars are frequent in this area . . ." I jerked my head at the entrance. "CCTV, unlikely they brought it out the door."

Dehan nodded and walked to the corner of Bryant. I followed her and we strolled down to the end of the block. There was an alleyway that led down the side of the brownstone to the church-yard. There was a gate with a padlock at the near end, and another where it connected with the church.

"What are you thinking?" She had her skeptical face on.

I smiled. "I'm not. I just want to know what the place looks like."

We walked back up Lafayette and made our way through the large iron gates that guarded the entrance to the House of the Almighty. There was a gravel path that led, among lawns, to the Gothic arch of the main door. To the left, attached to the main nave, was a house built in a similar style, also made of gray stone, though the gabled roof was of dark slate tiles. The door was a cheerful, fire-engine red, with a shiny brass knocker in the middle.

"What do you think?" I asked. "Is he at home having tea, or is he doing God's work?"

She didn't answer. Instead she followed me around the side of the church, through the grounds. There were a lot of trees, mainly plane trees, though there were some poplars and cypresses too.

"This was my mom's church," she said. "When I was a kid, we used to come here on Sundays."

A footpath ran along the side of the building. At the end, where the main body of the church ended, there was a sharp angle to the left. It had the depth of the nave, maybe forty or fifty feet, and formed another angle with an old redbrick building that looked as though it might have been a coach house or a stable. A number of fruit trees had been planted in the lee of the walls.

The footpath continued past this recess until the grass was

replaced with concrete, and two steps led down to the iron gate that we had seen at the end of the alleyway. I surveyed all this and asked, "Did your dad come with you?"

"No, he used to go to the synagogue."

We started back toward the front of the church. "How come you went with your mom and not your dad?"

"I went to both. Sometimes it was one week mom, one week dad. Sometimes it was months. They were never sure how to handle it and they were never sure how best to please God."

"I never got it," I said.

"Never got what?"

"Three religions, all devoted to the same god, all trying real hard to please him, and instead of being grateful, he gives all three of them a real hard time."

She gave a small laugh. "He gave the oil to the Muslims, the banks to the Jews, and the empires to the Christians, but the tortured souls He distributed evenly amongst all three."

We had reached the main entrance. The massive doors stood open onto an impenetrable darkness. I stood looking at the dark arch. "Do I gather you are an atheist?"

She shrugged. "Do I need a label? I read all the holy books and came to the conclusion they were all written by men. Mostly men who had been too long in the desert, suffering from dehydration." She looked at me with a bland smile. "Hydrate a man and put him in a lab, he will tend to talk more sense."

"Or a woman."

"There's that."

"I feel a disturbance in the Force. I think he is in the church, doing God's work."

We stepped through the portal into the cool, echoing darkness. Our footfalls seemed to slide up the walls and scamper around the vaulted ceilings. Two rows of arches supported on marble columns separated the aisles from the central nave. A red carpet led to the vast, golden altar, where archangels and saints stood watching, with apparent indifference, as Jesus, raised up on a vast wooden cross, continued his two-thousand-year ordeal of suffering and self-sacrifice.

There was a figure kneeling before the altar, dressed in black. He heard the echo of our feet approaching, and when we came to a halt behind him, he crossed himself and stood. As he turned, I said, "Father Padraig O'Neil?"

"That's my name." He smiled. We showed him our badges and told him whom we were. He remained impassive and asked, "How can I help you, Detectives?"

"Do you recall a young attorney who used to volunteer here about twelve years ago, name of Sean O'Conor?"

His face lit up. "Sean? Do I remember Sean? Well, of course I do! A rare and wonderful young man, but if you're looking for him, I'm afraid I have no idea where he is."

When Dehan spoke, she had a harshness to her voice that made me look up. "We're not looking for him, Father O'Neil. We'd like to talk to you about him. Is there somewhere we can speak, in private?"

He noticed her tone too and frowned slightly. "Of course, let's go through to the rectory, we can talk there."

He led us to a small wooden door at the end of the north transept. He unlocked it with an old, chub key and ushered us through.

The rectory had the same feeling of hushed reverence and contemplation as the church, but without the distant, vaulted echoes. We were in a broad, carpeted hallway with the front door on the left, probably the bright red one I had seen earlier. There were a couple of rooms up ahead with tenuous sunlight filtering through half-open doors, and a wide, solid mahogany staircase on the right that climbed to a landing over our heads.

Father O'Neil closed and locked the door behind us.

"I was going to have some tea." He smiled. "It's hard to shake the habits of the old country. Would you join me?"

Dehan said nothing, but I thanked him, and he asked us to go into the parlor while he spoke to Mrs. Doyle about a brew.

The parlor was large, comfortable, and old world. There was an open fireplace with a vase of chrysanthemums in it. An old TV stood pushed away in a corner on a trolley, attached to a DVD player and an old video machine. A large crucifix over the fireplace dominated the room. There was one bookcase, and most of the volumes were hardbacks on the subject of Catholic theology.

Two large, leather armchairs and a leather sofa were arranged around the fire. They looked out of place in that room, and expensive. I sat in one of the chairs and Dehan sat on the sofa.

Father O'Neil came bustling in in his cassock, muttering that "that was sorted," and settled himself in the remaining chair. He smiled at us each in turn and asked, "Now, how can I help you? You wanted to ask me about Sean?"

"Anything you can tell us, Father. I believe he did a lot of charitable work here."

He nodded vigorously. "Oh yes, indeed. He was one in a million. Nothing, nothing was too much trouble for him. He had a very good job over in Brooklyn, at a very distinguished law firm. But he devoted every spare minute of his time to helping those in need. He was a true Christian and no mistake."

Dehan was watching him like a cat watching a mouse hole.

I nodded. "Did he ever confide in you with regard to the cases he was handling?" He hesitated and I added, "In particular, the pro bono work he did on behalf of the needy."

His face became grave. "He did, Detective." He frowned at us both and looked confused. "But you must know that Sean has been missing for, oh . . . ten years at least."

Dehan said, "To be precise, Father, twelve years and three months. He went missing in January 2005."

He narrowed his eyes at her for a moment, then looked at me. "So you are looking into his disappearance?"

I weighed it up in my mind for a moment, made a decision, and said, "We are looking into his murder, Father."

"Oh, sweet Jesus . . ." He crossed himself and said a quick

prayer. "I had a feeling . . . When he just disappeared like that, with no explanation, it was just, not like him."

I waited. I felt Dehan glance at me. Finally, I said, "The cases, Father? We believe one of the cases he was working on might have had something to do with his death."

Mrs. Doyle came in carrying a tray and set it on a table by the window. She smiled at me as though she'd done something naughty but she knew I was going to let her off with a light spanking, and said, "Now, who's going to have a nice cup of tea, and some fresh biscuits? My own recipe—you can't say no!"

We all agreed we couldn't, and she took her sweet time distributing the fruits of her labor. When she left, Father O'Neil smiled beatifically after her and said, "Truly, I do not know what I would do without that woman."

Dehan dunked her biscuit as though she was trying to drown it and said, "Did Sean ever confide in you, Father, regarding any of the cases he was involved in just before his disappearance?"

He heaved a huge sigh.

I said, "I am beginning to get the impression, Father, that this is a subject you are uncomfortable discussing."

He grimaced at his tea, like he didn't really want it. "Of course you are quite right, Detective Stone, and I must apologize. The matter is not as simple as it might seem."

"What is it that makes it complicated?" I asked the question, but I was pretty sure I knew what the answer was going to be. He didn't disappoint me.

"The Irish community in the Bronx, in New York as a whole, is a complex one. There are many loyalties, and occasionally those loyalties come into conflict . . ."

Dehan said, "Can we move from generalities to specifics, Father?"

"Yes. He did confide in me, and seek my guidance, regarding some of the cases in which he was engaged. Especially those cases he took on which were on behalf of the needy."

"Is there any case in particular that he mentioned at that time, that you felt might have threatened his life?"

He looked sick and drained. "The Tiffany Street squat. Sean was brave to the point of recklessness. If he saw just one person suffering injustice, he had to act. He had to do something."

There was an edge to Dehan's voice. "Is there something wrong with that?"

"Of course not, except that life is rarely that simple. Conor Hagan is a very powerful and dangerous man. I am sure you are well aware of him, and what he is capable of." He gave a small laugh and nodded several times. "What people are less aware of is the good he does for the Irish community. Things are very rarely black and white, Detective Dehan."

"Putting people on the street doesn't sound much like benefiting the community. Or were they not Irish?"

He glanced at her resentfully. "Some of them were indeed Irish. Others were Mexican. There were people of all colors and races. But that was not the point. The point was that Conor Hagan was going to develop that plot for the benefit of the community. Perhaps he was not following the letter of the law, and perhaps people would have been made temporarily homeless . . ."

"In January, in New York."

"Indeed, but left to his own way of doing things, Conor would have made sure that those people he evicted were taken care of. But Sean, he had to play Galahad. He had to go charging in and upset the applecart." He saw the way we were looking at him and made a hasty retreat. "Don't get me wrong. I had the greatest admiration for Sean, and for everything he wanted to do. I just felt he might have gone about it in a more . . . circumspect way."

"It seems," I said, before Dehan could get in, "that you are suggesting that Conor Hagan might have killed Sean O'Conor, or at least had him killed."

His face went crimson and he began to laugh. "Well now, steady on! That is not in fact what I said."

"What are you saying, Father?"

"What I'm saying is that, the way Sean went charging in, where angels fear to tread, was liable to upset somebody, sooner or later."

Dehan snapped, "So he had it coming?"

"That is not what I meant!"

"I'll tell you what I think, Father O'Neil," I said. "I think that you are being vague and evasive because you don't want to go charging in where angels fear to tread. But I am going to be very clear with you, Father. If you are withholding evidence in a murder investigation in order to protect a killer, I will come gunning for you. And you may not believe it, but I am a much more dangerous man than Conor Hagan. Because if Conor Hagan is guilty of this murder, I will take him down, and if you conceal evidence, I will take you down too." I leered. "And believe me, if Hagan goes to prison, you really don't want to be in there with him."

He had both hands up, like I was pointing a gun at him. "Steady, lad! Slow down! This is getting a little out of hand. I never said I would not cooperate with you. I was simply trying to make you appreciate the complexity of the situation!"

"I appreciate the complexity of the situation. What I need to know now is whether Sean had received any concrete threats, if anybody from Hagan's organization had contacted him and told him to leave the case alone . . . was there anything specific that made Sean fear for his life?"

He thought about it for a long time, chewing his lip. Finally, he said, "A couple of days before he disappeared, he came to me and told me that he had received a number of threatening phone calls telling him to leave the case alone or face the consequences."

"Did he recognize the voice?"

"He didn't say so, but he was in no doubt that it was Hagan."

Dehan said, "And when he went missing, it never occurred to you to inform the police?"

He shook his head. "To be honest, I thought he had run off. I thought it had finally dawned on him that he had gone too far . . ."

Dehan said, "Gone too far? What does that mean?"

He flopped back in his chair. He was obviously embarrassed at his own cowardice. "Too far means, Hagan is much more than a man. If you put Conor or any of his henchmen in prison, there will be ten more behind him to take his place. And if he warns you off and you don't heed the warning at the time, you will be punished, and it's no good heeding the warning later. That's too late. If you do not toe the line, you will be punished."

Dehan's voice was scathing. "Does that apply to priests as well?"

He snapped, "Yes! And police officers!"

I said, "Good to know. So you thought that Sean had finally seen the light, but too late, and done a runner. What made you think that?"

He shrugged. "Well, there was no reason to believe any harm had come to him. If he had been hurt, there would have been some news, or a report or something, or a message from his parents. Also, didn't his fiancée go missing at the same time! I assumed they'd run off together."

Dehan sat forward. "Just so I can get this clear in my mind, Father, do I understand . . ." She shook her head and started again. "Are you telling us that when your parishioners come to you and ask you for guidance because they are being bullied, abused, and threatened by gangsters, you advise them to toe the line, look the other way, and keep quiet?"

His face flushed and suddenly he looked mad. "Well, what do you suggest I tell them, Detective? To go to the police? Because for your information, a good number of you are on Hagan's payroll, and I, personally, have never accepted money or gifts from him, but if I ever oppose him or confront him, it will not be I who suffers! It will be them, the parishioners. He has made that abundantly clear to me, and that was what I tried to make Sean understand!"

I sat forward. "Well, it wasn't the parishioners who paid, Father O'Neil, it was Sean. And you did get news, only you didn't realize it."

"What are you talking about?"

"Do you remember a tramp, a vagrant, whose body was found in a dumpster at the end of the road at the very same time that Sean went missing?"

His mouth dropped and he stared from me to Dehan and back again. "Don't . . . Surely you're not telling me . . ."

I nodded. "We won't take up any more of your time, Father. But before we go, did you say his fiancée went missing at the same time?"

"I assumed they had eloped together."

"What was her name? I'd like to try and trace her."

He heaved a big sigh and sank back in his chair. "Poor child, I suppose now this means . . . Sweet Jesus, it doesn't bear thinking about . . ."

"Her name, Father?"

"I'm trying to remember." He looked me in the eye. "Alice. Alicia Flores."

Dehan said, "Alicia Flores Delgado?"

He stared at her. "Yes, that's her. Did you know her? Are you from this neighborhood? You do look familiar."

"Yeah, I'm from the hood." She didn't sound friendly when she said it.

I asked him, "Do you have a phone number or an address for her parents or next of kin?"

He went to rise but Dehan said, "I know where they live."

I stood. "Thank you, Father, you have been very helpful. We may need to talk to you again."

He spread his hands and gestured at the building around him. "I'm not going anywhere."

He saw us to the door, and we stepped out into the gathering dusk.

FIVE

WE DROVE IN SILENCE ALONG BRUCKNER BOULEVARD AS far as Castle Hill Avenue and then turned left over the bridge and stopped at Jimmy's. All the way she was trying not to scowl, although all the way she scowled.

The evening crowd wasn't in yet, and we found a quiet table near the corner. As we moved toward it, I called to Jimmy and held up two fingers, like the peace sign. When the beers arrived and Jimmy had left, I said, "You going to tell me what's going on?"

She did that thing where she gave her head a couple of small shakes and made a "no idea what you're talking about" face while avoiding eye contact. I persisted.

"Is it something I said or did that has annoyed you?"

This time she looked down at her drink, shook her head, and made a "no, that's ridiculous" face.

"Is it something related to the case?"

She closed her eyes and sighed.

"Then you have to tell me, Dehan."

"So you can take me off the case?"

I drank and wiped the foam from my mouth with the back of my hand. "Only if it impairs your ability to perform your duty."

She drew breath, but before she could speak I went on, "And if you don't tell me what's going on, I'll have no choice but to conclude it has impaired your ability, because you will be keeping relevant information from me. Tell me what's on your mind, and trust me to make the right choice, Carmen."

She scowled, curled her lip, and spoke through gritted teeth. "You're so feckin' reasonable!"

"Ah, Jaysus! Isn't that the truth after all! Now, spill."

She heaved another sigh, leaned back in her chair, and stared me in the eye. "Alicia Flores Delgado was my cousin."

She watched me while I stared at my beer, then at the wall, and then out the window, where the air was turning from dusk to dark. Finally, I asked her, "Did you know that Sean was her fiancée? Before?"

She shook her head. "No, we were very close as kids, but as we got older . . ." She shrugged. "She got involved in the church . . . that wasn't my scene."

I believed her. "Is there anything else? Anything you're not telling me?"

She thought about it, then shook her head again. "No."

I leaned forward and stared hard at her. "I want you to keep me in the loop every inch of the way, you understand me?"

"Yeah, of course." She nodded.

I shook my head. "No, not 'of course.' I mean it, as your partner and as your friend. Do you understand me?"

Her face changed. She looked grateful, though she tried to hide it.

"Yeah, I understand you. Thanks."

I sucked my teeth for a moment, reflecting that this case was becoming complicated. His hair and nails had told me it would from the start, but this I had not anticipated, and I was wondering where to start.

"What did you mean, she 'was' your cousin?" It was as good a place as any.

She kind of shrugged with one shoulder and shook her head.

"You'd have to know Alicia. She was . . ." She searched for the right words and suddenly expostulated, "She was everything I am not! She was the quintessential good girl. She was sweet, always ready with a smile, good-natured, could never do enough to help . . ." She paused, holding my eye. She looked real sad. "And she would never—not in a thousand years—she would never just up and go without telling her family where she was going. It just isn't credible. Her family was everything to her, and if she hasn't contacted them, it's because she can't . . ."

She left the words hanging, ugly with meaning.

"I can see why Hagan would want Sean O'Conor out of the way. Hell, I can see that it would be an imperative for him to make an example of Sean. But Alicia?" I thought about it and Dehan, nodding, spoke my thoughts. "Alicia would only make sense if Sean was still alive."

"Exactly. Her only value to Hagan is as leverage with Sean, or as a way of punishing him."

She sighed. "It doesn't make a lot of sense. The Irish Mob are about as tough as they get, but they have a reverence for family, and for women. A good Catholic girl like that, active in the church . . . I don't see it."

She was right. "We need to talk to Alicia's family."

She shifted her position, leaned back, and crossed her long legs at the ankle on the side stretcher of my chair. She nodded absently and said, "So what are we saying, then? Sean O'Conor has a Galahad complex. He gets involved in the charitable work at St. Mary's, and at the same time gets into this Drop-In Center, offering pro bono legal representation. He decides to take a swing at the big guy, Conor Hagan. Conor executes him, for some reason he dresses him as a tramp and throws him in one of his own dumpsters, right by the church. Maybe it was a message to the local population. And then . . ."

She went into a kind of daze, staring at her boots.

I said, "Maybe she committed suicide?"

She pulled a face. "Where's the body?"

"Jumped off the Bruckner Expressway into the river?"

"Without being seen?"

A human body is not an easy thing to lose, or to hide, especially when it's dead. Live humans are a lot easier to conceal and camouflage. Dead ones just keep doing embarrassing, awkward things like decomposing, smelling, and generally looking out of place. It is very difficult for a dead body simply to vanish. Which was what Alicia seemed to have done.

"Also," I said, "Why leave Sean in full view, and dispose of Alicia so that no one will find her?"

As I said it, I knew that was an important question, and by the way Dehan looked at me, she did too.

I held up the fingers of my left hand and enumerated.

"First, tomorrow morning we go and visit Alicia's parents, set that up tonight if you can. Second, after that, we pay a visit to Conor Hagan, see what he has to say about the Tiffany Street squatters. Third, we go through the contents from Sean's room with a fine-tooth comb. There is something here we are missing."

She pointed at me like she was going to shoot me with her finger.

"Different motives, but it would be too bizarre for it to be coincidence. So, same killer, same overall crime, but different personal motives."

I nodded. It made sense.

I HAD BEEN EXPECTING IT. So when I was awakened from my sleep by the incessant ringing on my doorbell, I wasn't surprised or alarmed. I groped for my keys in my pants pocket and leaned out the window. It was cold and still dark. The sun wouldn't be up for another half hour at least. Dehan was doing her cold weather dance and grinned at me. "They are early risers," she said.

I threw the key down to her and groped my way to the bathroom.

As was her custom, when I got downstairs she was frying bacon and eggs and making coffee. I sat at the kitchen table.

"Did you sleep?"

She gave her head a quick shake. "No."

The toast popped. She buttered it and shoveled bacon from the pan onto the plate with a spatula. Then she broke the eggs into the pan.

"When we were small, we were like sisters, always in and out of each other's houses. Her parents didn't care that my dad was a Jew."

I blinked. These were big issues for before coffee. But she didn't need an answer, now she was shoveling eggs.

"These days, Jews and Christians are uniting against Islam, a common enemy, but not so long ago Catholics hated Jews about as much as Muslims do."

She put two huge plates of eggs and bacon on toast on the table. She had even found some mushrooms and fried those too. She went back for two cups and the coffeepot. She was still talking.

"But Alicia's parents weren't like that. Gregorio and Marcela. They were good people, you know what I mean?" She sat and attacked her food with a kind of determination to get the job done. "And I was thinking about that all night. How do you know a person is good? I mean, really good?" She glanced at me as she stuffed food into her mouth. It didn't stop her talking. "I meam, whadish goom, righ?"

"What is good?"

She nodded. I sipped my coffee, hoping it would give me strength, and speared a rasher of bacon. She swallowed, as though she was getting the food out of the way of her stream of thoughts.

"Yeah. Nobody has ever been able to define good or evil. It's one of those things, like love. You can't define it. But we know, don't we, when a person is good. We know when they are false, hypocrites, on an ego trip—and we know when they are genuinely good." She waved her knife at me. "Me? I'm just confused. You, you're basically a good guy who is smart and has learnt to be careful. Gregorio, Marcela, and Alicia, they were genuine good people."

She was starting to carry me along with her relentless flow. I said, "That's a lot of genuinely good people: Sean, Gregorio, Marcela, and Alicia. What are the odds?"

"Astronomical. But you get enough monkeys with typewriters, one of them will write the Torah. The point is, they found each other, they came together, and they tried to do good. Sean was a kind of catalyst for them, do you see that, Stone? His energy, his conviction, his faith—whatever! He acted as a catalyst and they started to do something to bring about change. And that is why they died. It's wrong, Stone. They—people like Conor Hagan—they own the world, and they can't be allowed to keep getting away with this kind of shit."

"You didn't sleep at all?"

"No. You done?"

"No, I am still mopping and I still have my coffee. Your revs are too high. Let in the clutch and breathe."

"It makes me mad, Stone."

"I can see that."

"Why?"

"Why can I see that?"

"No. Why do they get away with it?"

"I don't know. It's the nature of the world we live in."

"It shouldn't be."

I drew breath, looked at her, and killed my reply before I said it. She had tears in her eyes as I reached across the table and gave her hand a squeeze. "We do the best we can, Carmen. It's all we can do."

The horizon was turning pale and the dawn chorus was in full swing as we stepped into the street. There was a fresh, green smell of hope in the air. Somewhere in the distance, a car radio was giving the weather report for the day, and a bus, grinding through its gears, ferried yawning people from slumber to morning. Hope,

I thought to myself, was it one of those things that Dehan had talked about, like good and evil, and love? Something you couldn't define, but you knew it was there.

I sighed and climbed into the car. I was no good with all that abstract stuff. I was good at getting the job done, and that was exactly what I planned to do.

SIX

GREGORIO WAS STILL AT WORK. HE DID THE NIGHT shift, but Marcela was home. They had the top floor of a double fronted house on Irvine Street, near the corner of Garrison Avenue. We climbed the stairs to the top floor, where a plaster-board wall had been put in to turn what should have been a family home into two apartments. Once the wall was up, some-body had started to paint it but given up halfway. The landing was big enough for just one person. Dehan went ahead and rang the bell.

Marcela was short, overweight, and pretty. Dehan had to stoop to hug her, and winced at the shriek of pleasure the woman let out in her ear. They babbled in Spanish while I waited on the stairs, and Marcela kept coming in for follow-up hugs and kisses. Finally, Dehan turned and said, "Marcela, this is John, he's my partner."

She dragged Dehan into the apartment so she could get at me, gave me two big kisses on my cheeks, and told me how handsome I was in two languages. Then she pushed us both into her living room.

They sat together on the sofa and Marcela pinched her cheek and squeaked, "*Ay, mi Carmencita preciosa!*"

Dehan smiled and held her hand in both of her own. "*Tita*, we need to talk to you. It is really important."

Marcela became serious. "Is this police business?"

"It's about Alicia, *Tita*."

Marcela put her hands to her cheeks and gasped. "*Ay Dios mío!* Did you find her? Is she okay? Did something happen to her?"

"We don't know yet, but we found Sean."

"You found Sean?" She could tell from Dehan's face that it wasn't good news. "Is he dead?"

Dehan nodded. "Yes, *Tita*, he was murdered twelve years ago, when he disappeared."

Marcela's face drained white. "So, Alicia . . . ?"

Dehan reached quickly for her hand. "No, *Tita*, not necessarily. We don't know what happened to Alicia. Sean's body was there all along, right by the church, *tu me entiendes*? But nobody recognized it because they changed his clothes. But Alicia, there was no body found anywhere, so maybe she escaped. Maybe she went away where they couldn't find her."

There were tears in Marcela's eyes. "She would call. She would tell me where she was."

"Not if she was trying to protect you."

"Protect me? Who from?"

"That's what we need to find out, *Tita*."

I sat forward. "Marcela, did Sean come to your house often?"

Her face lit up. "Oh, yes, all the time. Such a nice boy, very handsome and so kind. They were going to get married."

"How did he and Alicia meet?"

"At the church. He was a good Christian. Very *devoto*." She gave a cheeky smile. "Maybe too much, huh? I think maybe I never get grandchildren!" She laughed uproariously, slapping Dehan on the leg.

I smiled. "And Alicia was also a good Catholic, right?"

She clasped her hands to her heart and cocked her head. "So

good, such a good child. Loved her mammy, didn't she, Carmencita?"

"She sure did, *Tita.*"

"So, what was Alicia doing at the church, Marcela?"

She shrugged and pulled a face. "The soup kitchen, distributin' the clothes for the poor people. 'Cause it gets real cold for the homeless people in the winter. She work with the *huerfanitos* . . ."

"The what?"

"The little orphan children. Some of them, their parents have died, others their parents have gone to prison, or they can't care for them because they drinkin' or takin' drugs, you know? These kids got nowhere to go, no school, nowhere to live."

"And Alicia helped them? How?"

"Father O'Neil is a good man." She turned reprovingly to look at Dehan. "I know you don't like him, but he is a good man." She looked back to me. "He organize classes for the kids to learn reading and writing, math, the basic things you gonna need, and he provide a place for them to sleep and stay when is cold."

"And Alicia was involved in this program?"

"Involve? She run it! She was runnin' the program, and Sean was trying to get compensation for the eviction on Tiffany Street. They were both really trying to help the community. Like two saints." She started to cry. "But they was too good, and God take them to his bosom. Lord know we need people like this in the world. Why he takes them away?"

Dehan put her arms around her and held her. "We don't know he did, Marcela. Let's wait and see, okay?"

"Marcela, we only have a couple more questions."

She blew her nose and nodded at me.

"Did he ever talk about what he was doing? Did he ever mention any people, any names?"

She rolled her eyes and threw her hands up in the air. "*Ay!* Always! Always! He was talking about Conor Hagan. He was obsessed with Conor Hagan. I tell him, 'Sean, there are more bad guys in the world than Conor Hagan!' but he don' wanna know. He is obsess, he gonna bring him down and punish him for the bad things he done. I tell him, 'Back off a little or you gonna get problems,' but he don't listen to me." She paused a moment to fold her handkerchief. "A week or a few days before he disappear, he come and he say to Alicia, 'They callin' me, warning me to back off,' they are tryin' to buy him off and threatening him. He said to her, 'You want we can split up, so you and your family are not at risk?' She said no, she was gonna stand by him. That is the kind of girl she is."

"So Sean told Alicia he had received threats from Conor Hagan?"

"Oh yeah, for sure."

Dehan held her hand tight. "*Tita*, have you got anything—letters, emails, a computer, a cell phone, anything from back then that might have something on it that we can use . . ."

"You mean like proof?" She shrugged and shook her head. "No, *cielito*, I ain't got nothing. She never had no computer, and her phone disappear with her. That day, she go to the church like always, and she never come back."

She insisted we have coffee; we talked some more without making any progress and finally made our way back to the car. I leaned on the roof and sighed. The morning was bright and optimistic, but I wasn't.

Dehan opened her door, stopped, and leaned opposite me. We stared at each other. She said, "Everything confirms the same hypothesis. It's simple and logical. Maybe we're overthinking it."

"Maybe, but some concrete evidence would be nice. And I still don't like Sean in a dumpster and Alicia vanishing without a trace. It doesn't make sense."

"I know."

"Let's see if the tech guys got anything from Sean's computer, and let's have a look through his papers. You never know, there might be something. I'd like to have a little more than theories and hearsay before I confront Hagan."

She nodded and we got in.

SEVEN

Spring is real ugly and depressing when it's on the other side of the glass and you're sitting, wading through twelve-year-old legal notes about people getting evicted from their homes.

The only thing the tech guys were able to tell me at that stage was what I already suspected: the hard drive had been wiped clean. They were working on trying to recover some of the files, but they didn't want to make any promises. Twelve years was a long time.

Most of the physical files he had stored in two large sports bags in his wardrobe, and most of them related to cases from the previous year. Hard as we looked, we could barely find a single reference to Tiffany Street, Conor Hagan, or squatters. Dehan spoke absently as she leafed slowly through a notebook.

"It's negative, but even that is pointing in the same direction. They killed him and Alicia, then they went and took his files and wiped his PC."

I took the last file from the bag. I had seen several like it. It was about Carolina, a child of thirteen. Her dad was unknown; her mother was a prostitute and a junkie. Her nationality was unknown, and she apparently had no Social Security number.

Cristina, twelve, wasn't sure where her mother was. Sean was trying to get them both taken into care. He was also trying to get the authorities to recognize there was a crisis with this kind of child in the Bronx. Meanwhile, Father O'Neil was providing them with somewhere to sleep and somewhere to eat, and Alicia was providing lessons in basic literacy and numeracy.

I threw the file on the desk and rubbed my face with my hands.

"What am I not seeing, Dehan? What am I missing? Everything is perfect. We should just be looking for hard evidence, witnesses, forensics—but there is something missing."

She nodded. "I agree."

"What the hell did they do with Alicia, and for what purpose?" I stood and walked to the window, looking out resentfully at April having fun out there, budding all the almond trees. "Sean and Alicia . . . no, just Sean, who became a pain in Hagan's ass. Alicia wasn't. As far as we know, Dehan, Hagan doesn't even know Alicia exists, and so he has a couple of his guys wait for Sean. They bundle him in the back of a car and take him to a building site or a warehouse. They put him on his knees and they shoot him."

I paused, running through it again in my mind. Dehan closed the file she was reading and turned her chair so she could see me. I went on.

"So far it is a bog-standard, textbook gangland hit. But then, for some reason, they take all his clothes off, dress him up as a tramp, take him to their own dumpster, and throw him in."

Dehan sighed. "It's a reach, Stone, but maybe Hagan wanted the locals to know about it, but, like we said before, he wanted it to go cold for the cops."

I nodded. "It's the only explanation that makes sense for now, but you're right, it's a reach." I wandered back to my chair and stood looking down at the file on the desk, thinking of Alicia, and Carolina and Cristina and their junkie mom. "And then, for no apparent reason, they go and find Alicia, kill her, and dispose of the body in such a way that nobody will ever find it." I turned and stared at her. "What the hell for?"

"As a warning?"

"To whom? Alicia was no threat to anybody. And you heard yourself, whatever else Hagan was, he also liked to play benefactor to the community; surely he would want to encourage people like Alicia, not kill them." I shook my head. "No, he had a very particular reason to kill her, and to make her disappear."

She thought about it.

"That's a pretty strong statement, Sensei."

"But it's the only thing that makes sense."

She sighed and threw her own file on the desk. "Well, we are going to have to find some evidence pretty soon, Stone, because we are hitting one dead end after another." She stretched, arching her back over the back of the chair till I heard the vertebrae crack. "Maybe you should talk to Hagan."

I shook my head. "I don't want to. It's too soon. That guy is going to be tough and cool. I need something concrete before I go up against him."

I picked up the empty bag off the floor, dumped it on the desk, and put a handful of files back in it. The weight was badly distributed; it overbalanced and slid to the floor. Dehan snorted and grinned. "One of those days."

I bent and retrieved the bag. The files slid to the end. I put the bag back with more care. The base was soft, floppy, that was why it had overbalanced and slid off the desk. But there was something odd about it. I picked it up again by the handles and lowered it gently onto the edge of the desk. It buckled. I raised it and lowered it again, but a bit further along. It didn't buckle. I took the files out and dropped them on the floor. Then tipped the bag back and forth in a seesaw motion. Dehan was watching me like she thought I had finally lost it and was ready for sectioning.

I said, "Listen . . ." I tipped the bag again. There was a slithering sound. "There is something in there."

I put it back on the table, pulled my penknife from my

pocket, and gently cut away the bottom of the bag. And there it was, a thick A4 file.

"Holy shit, Stone."

I threw the bag on the floor. She stood and came to stand beside me. I put the file on the desk and opened it, and there were thirteen color photographs. A4 size. The first was a group of twelve kids; they were in a large room that was hard to identify. It had a burgundy carpet and you could make out what looked like a white, wooden windowsill on the far left. The kids were standing in a group. They were all girls of varying ages, the youngest about twelve, and the oldest about fifteen. They all looked Latin American.

I set that photograph aside and looked at the next one. My skin went cold. It was one of the girls from the group. She was nude. She was sitting on a bed, smiling, but the smile, and her eyes, showed fear. Real fear. She was smiling because she had to. I went through the rest, one photograph after another, with a black rage building inside me. Each of the kids in the group was photographed individually in the same way.

"We have to get these copied and sent to the lab for fingerprints."

"What the fuck does it mean?"

"It means Sean O'Conor was involved in more than protecting squatters' rights."

She stared at me. "You think these were Sean's pictures?"

I shook my head. "I didn't say that. We don't know whose they are, but what is certain is that they provide a powerful motive for murder. They provide several powerful motives for murder."

She walked slowly back to her chair while I copied the pictures and sealed them in a plastic envelope for the forensic lab. She sat.

"This complicates things a lot, Stone."

I nodded. "Talk me through it."

She thought for a moment. "One, he found Hagan was not

only screwing the squatters, he was running a child prostitution ring."

I nodded. "Okay."

She held up a hand. "This makes sense, because if Hagan was preying on the homeless kids, on orphans, on the very kids Father O'Neil and Alicia were trying to help, suddenly he has a reason to kill her. Father O'Neil he can intimidate, but Alicia, encouraged by Sean's support, defies him. So he kills her along with Sean."

I nodded again. "It's a possible scenario. What else?"

She frowned. "What else? You don't like that?"

I raised an eyebrow at her. "I love it, but what else?"

She sighed. "Okay, she discovers that Father O'Neil, intimidated by Hagan, is running a child pornography ring; she goes to Sean with evidence, they confront him, and he goes to Hagan, who has them both killed."

I shrugged. "What else?"

She spread her hands. "What else . . . ?"

"Neither of your two scenarios explains why Alicia disappeared. You are assuming that the photographs are Sean's evidence against somebody." She didn't like it and her face said so, so I went on. "So what would Alicia do if she discovered that her perfect man was into child pornography?"

She looked at me like she wanted to hit me.

"Kill him and disappear."

I shook my head. "But I don't like it. It explains why she disappears, but it doesn't explain Sean dressed as a tramp in a dumpster."

"So why . . . ?" She looked exasperated.

"Because, young grasshopper, you discard a hypothesis after you explore it, not before. Just because Sean seems to be a nice guy, it does not mean he has no dark secrets."

"Yes, Sensei . . ."

"Come on, let's get these to the lab."

EIGHT

On the way, Dehan phoned Hagan Construction and made an appointment to see Conor Hagan. His secretary said he was out of town, but he would be in his office the following day at noon, if we wanted to come and see him then. Dehan said we did.

By the time we'd left the photographs at the lab, it was lunchtime, so we grabbed a couple of hot dogs and sat on the hood of my car eating them. Dehan was licking ketchup from her fingers with the concentration of a cat. As she did it, she asked, "What now?"

I crammed the tail end of the sausage dog into my maw and said, "I shink I bonch dishtur paja O'Neesh runsh."

She stopped licking and considered me a moment, while I too licked ketchup from my fingers.

"You want to disturb Father O'Neil's lunch . . ."

"Mm-hm!"

I fished my cell out of my pocket and made the call.

"Father O'Neil, it's Detective Stone here again."

He didn't sound elated. "Detective Stone, yes, how may I help you?"

"A couple of unexpected things have come up, Father, and I need to ask you a few more questions."

"Of course."

"Shall I send a car for you, or can you get to the precinct yourself?"

There was a stunned silence. Then, "You want me to . . ."

"That's the idea."

"I see, well, yes, of course. I have a lot to do here . . ."

I gave him my best dead, toneless voice and said, "I can send a car for you."

"No, that won't be necessary."

"Shall we say half an hour?"

He said he thought he could manage that, and we headed back to the 43rd.

I took the long way home, via Eastchester and Silver Street. I had never liked the original theory on Sean's murder. It was too easy and left too many unanswered questions. But the photographs had confused the picture even more, and I was having trouble putting the puzzle together in my head. As we turned onto East Tremont Avenue, Dehan said, "You were pretty tough on Father O'Neil back there."

"You think I was wrong?"

"No, I'm just curious."

I nodded. After a moment, I said, "You weren't real warm toward him yourself when we went to see him."

"You answering my question with a question of your own?"

I smiled. "He's hiding something. He's scared of Hagan. I want him to be more scared of me than he is of Hagan. So what's your beef with him?"

She didn't answer straightaway. She stared out the side window at the redbrick and concrete desolation, the steel, roll-down shutters sprayed with unoriginal graffiti, and the broad, open spaces of blacktop and sidewalk that nature had intended for meadows and woodlands, but Man had decreed should be artificial desert. She spoke suddenly, without looking at me.

"My mom went to him for help and guidance, a long time ago. Everything he said this morning was an echo of what he said to her back then. Don't fight, don't defend yourself or your family, accept your fate and surrender to those who abuse you. Pray for forgiveness."

I turned into Castle Hill. A few small leaves tinged the dead branches with green in the fragile sunlight of the early afternoon.

"What happened?"

She shook her head.

I glanced at her. That was the only answer I was going to get. I said, "That about sums it up. With a man like Father O'Neil, you can be pretty sure he's in Hagan's pocket. He is influential enough in the community to be of use, and scared enough not to face up to him. The million-dollar question is, what is the point beyond which Father O'Neil will not go?"

"You think there is one?"

"Sure. I don't read him as a bad guy, do you? I think he's weak, but I think he'd rather do good than not."

She shrugged.

I followed Castle Hill down to Bruckner Boulevard and turned right over the bridge. Five minutes later, I was pulling up outside the station. As Dehan was opening the door, I said, "You going to be okay in this interview?"

"Sure. Why not?"

"We both know there's stuff you are not telling me, Dehan. You have an issue with Father O'Neil. I'm not pushing you to tell me what it is, but I need to know you're going to be objective."

"I'll be objective."

Father O'Neil was already there. He'd been shown into an interview room and was sitting there fiddling with a paper cup of coffee. He looked up as we came in and smiled nervously.

"Detectives, I must confess I am a little surprised . . ."

He probably expected me to apologize and explain. Instead, I sat, dropped a file in front of me, and waited for him to finish his sentence. He didn't. He trailed off and glanced at Dehan, then back at me. When he didn't say anything, I asked him, "Father, what is the nature of your relationship with Conor Hagan?"

He frowned. "My . . ." He turned to look at Dehan again, as though he suspected the question had been her idea. Then he looked back at me. "My relationship . . . ?"

"Is there something about the question you don't understand, Father?"

"Well, I have no relationship with Conor Hagan."

I shook my head. "No, you have some kind of relationship, Father. I am asking you about the nature of that relationship. How long have you been the parish priest here?"

He felt he was on safer ground here and smiled.

"More than thirty years, Detective. And if you want to talk about relationships, the relationship I have built up with the parish over those years is one of mutual love and respect. We have run many, many programs, with the help and support of the parishioners, to assist the needy and the homeless, to . . ."

"I am aware of that, Father. Is Conor Hagan one of your parishioners?"

He nodded. "Yes, indeed he is."

"He must have been a young child when you took over as parish priest. You may even have christened him."

He was silent for a moment, studying his coffee. "Not quite," he said at last, "but he was a very small boy. His parents were, and still are, devout Catholics, and I have watched him grow into a man."

"Not quite accurate to say you have no relationship with him?"

He sighed and met my eye. "I have the same relationship with Conor that I have with any one of my parishioners, Detective."

I nodded. "I see. I'd like to know a little more about these programs you run. What is their main focus?"

He was a little more cautious this time, but again he felt on safer ground. He didn't like the subject of Conor Hagan.

"Mainly it's the children. Not exclusively—there are many,

many lost souls in the Bronx, Detective, as I am sure you are well aware. We care for the homeless as best we can, providing shelter and clothes and food. We provide help for women who . . ."

He hesitated and Dehan said, "Whores."

He stared at her, a little aghast, then nodded and said, "Women who have lost their way. Many are addicted to drugs, or live in fear of their boyfriends, or the men who . . ."

"Their pimps."

"Yes, thank you, Detective Dehan, but our main concern must be the children. For them, we have shelter, clothes, and food, and we also do our best to provide them with schooling, even if it is just basic literacy."

I drummed my fingers on the table a moment. "This was the program that Alicia was involved in."

"The blessed child was instrumental in setting it up."

"Who funds these programs? Even with volunteers, something like this requires money."

His face went hard. He said, "Donations," and clamped his jaw shut.

I waited. Dehan sighed and said, "Donations from whom, Father."

"There isn't a single donor . . ."

I snapped, "We can find out. It will take longer, but we will find out. I already have the feeling you are holding back information, Father, do you want to compound that feeling or do you want to cooperate with us?"

He drew breath, but Dehan was in before he could speak.

"What is it you are trying to hide?"

"I am not trying to hide anything!"

"So who funds these programs?"

"I told you! All sorts of people!"

"This morning you were at pains to stress that Conor Hagan does a lot to help the community. Is he one of your contributors?"

He sighed, and it was shaky. "Of course."

"Does he fund the orphan program?"

"Amongst others."

"He, amongst others? Or he funds that program, amongst others?"

It took him a surprisingly long time to answer.

"He funds that program, amongst others."

"Who else contributes to the orphan program?"

He hesitated. "Off the top of my head, collections from the parish, Conor, a couple of local businessmen."

"Names?"

"Sadiq Khan."

I stared at him in silence. Eventually, Dehan said, "Excuse me?"

"Sadiq Khan, he runs a shipping company . . ."

Dehan leaned forward. "Is he a convert to Catholicism?"

". . . No."

"He is a Muslim, then."

"I assume so, we have never discussed his religious beliefs."

Her voice was becoming tense, but I was curious to see where this would lead. "You never questioned the fact that a Muslim was funding a Catholic charity for orphans, in which the children were taught in the Christian faith?"

"Detective! It is not for me to question his motives! If he helps our children, then I am grateful. We both worship the same god, after all!"

"So the bottom line is," I said, "that this orphan charity is funded by Conor Hagan and Sadiq Khan."

"Yes, that is correct."

I sat back. "Not exactly 'all sorts of people,' is it, Father?"

"I suppose not."

I opened the folder and slid a photograph in front of him. It was the photo of the twelve kids standing together. His jaw dropped.

"Holy mother of God . . . !"

Dehan raised an eyebrow. "Do you know these children?"

He nodded. "Yes, but how . . . ?"

"How what, Father?" She leaned forward, staring at his face. "How did we get the photograph?"

He nodded again, staring at the picture. He picked it up and surprised me by smiling. He pointed. "Look, that is little Mati, this one is Jennifer . . . That little one with the cheeky grin, now what was her name? I'm pretty sure she was dyslexic, poor love. Sole, I am pretty sure it was Sole . . ."

"Who are these children, Father?"

He looked up at me, surprised, a little irritated.

"Sure, this is Alicia's first class. Isn't that why you're showing it to me?"

Dehan frowned. "They are all girls."

"Well, of course they are, Detective Dehan! We segregate the boys from the girls, especially at that age! How else are you going to teach them? Have you ever seen a Catholic school that didn't?"

I could feel the rage building in her, and I acted before she could open her mouth. I slid the next photograph in front of him.

"Is this also standard practice in Catholic schools, Father O'Neil?"

"Oh, sweet Jesus!"

He tried to stand, staggering back as he did so. The chair toppled and he fell over the chair, sprawling on the floor. He was struggling to his feet as Dehan and I moved around the table. His breathing was quick and ragged and he was holding out his left hand, like he was trying to ward off the photograph. He kept saying, "What . . . ? What . . . ?"

Dehan picked up his chair and I took his arm.

He was staring into my face. "What is that?"

I raised my eyebrows at him as I guided him back to the chair.

"It is a picture of a naked child, Father; one of the children in your orphan program, funded by Conor Hagan and Sadiq Khan, and run by you."

"No."

He said it as he sat. He refused to look at the picture and said again, "No."

I sat too, but Dehan remained standing, leaning on the back of her chair.

"What do you mean, 'No'?"

His voice was shrill. "What are these pictures? Where did they come from? Who took them? Who did this?"

I spoke quietly. "I was hoping you would tell me that."

"Jesus, Mary, and sweet Joanna! How in the name of all that is holy should I know?"

Dehan's voice was harsh. "You don't like to upset Conor, do you, Father?"

He was shaking his head, staring at her like she was a dangerous lunatic.

"You can't think . . ."

"It's a profitable racket."

"No!"

"What do you get out of it, Father?"

"No, no!"

"Or maybe all you have to do is look the other way, advise the kids to accept God's will and pray for his forgiveness. Is that what you do?"

"No! No, no, no, and a thousand times no!"

He'd managed to silence us. He stared furiously at us in the ringing silence. "You are wrong! I don't know what this filth is, but it has nothing to do with me, and I can tell you it has nothing to do with Conor!"

Dehan's voice was heavy with scorn. "He sticks to the moral high ground of extortion and drug trafficking, does he?"

Father O'Neil was shaking and his face was flushed. He leaned across the table, thrusting his face at Dehan. "Listen to me! I will admit that I try to keep the peace with people like Conor. It would take a much braver, and a much cleverer man than I to run that church, with as many charitable programs as I have, without a deal of give-and-take with the criminal community. Because the whole damned community is the criminal community! And if I don't toe the line, Detective, then people's legs get broken and people die!" He pointed a furious finger at her. "So don't come to me with your holier-than-thou airs and bloody graces! Before you lecture me on morality, young lady, you come down to Lafayette and run that church for six months, and tell me you never made a deal or an accommodation!"

We were quiet for a moment while he breathed and got a grip. Dehan spoke softly. "I lived in that neighborhood for twenty years; there is nothing you can tell me about it that I don't know."

He nodded, staring at the tabletop, and then raised his face to look at her.

"And how many people came to you for guidance and help? What do you tell a woman who comes to you weeping, Detective, saying that a gang member wants her for his girlfriend, he wants to have sexual intercourse with her, but she doesn't want to? She asks you for guidance and you know . . ." He raised his hand and pointed at her again. "You know that if you tell her to say no, he will kill her, or her husband, or her children! What advice do you give that woman? When the whole community looks to you for guidance, and you know that if you guide them on the right path, the repercussions to them will be death, brutality, and violence, what do you do?"

I looked at Dehan to see if she would answer. Her eyes were shining with anger, but she had no answer for him. I looked back at him and said, "You call the cops, Father O'Neil."

He burst out laughing. There was something manic to it.

"The police, is it? Is that the answer?" His face twisted suddenly into a mask of rage. "And what, Detective Stone, when it is the police doing the murdering and the raping? Whom do you call then?" He stood. "I have no idea who took these disgusting photographs, Detective, but I can tell you categorically that it was not me and it was not Conor. He may be a gangster, but he is not a twisted pervert." He pointed at the stack of photos in front of me. "For that kind of filth, maybe you should look closer to home!"

And with that he walked out.

We both sat in silence for a good thirty seconds. Finally, Dehan said, "What did he mean by that, Stone? What did he mean, closer to home?"

I pulled the photographs back across the table, careful only to touch the rim, and stared at them awhile.

"What do you think he meant?" I said.

NINE

THE DOOR OPENED AND A UNIFORMED SERGEANT leaned his head in.

"Detective, you have a call from the lab. He has been trying to reach you on your cell."

"Thanks, Sanchez. I'll call him back."

I dialed Frank's number and put it on speaker.

"Stone, I've been trying to reach you. It's about the computer."

"What have you got, Frank?"

"Not much, I'm afraid. Twelve years is a long time, but we managed to salvage a couple of emails and what appears to be part of a list. Some of the names had deteriorated beyond salvaging, but I've left two that were partly intact because they had recognizable letters remaining. I've sent the files to you. The emails are interesting, you'll see why straightaway, but I'm not sure how useful they'll be."

"Thanks. Any word on the photos?"

"Yes, the word is, I am not Harry Potter. I'll have something for you as soon as I can get to them."

"Thanks, Frank. I did mention it was child prostitution, didn't I?"

There was a pause.

"I'll get onto it straightaway."

"Good. I'm sending something else over to you for comparison."

While I was talking, Dehan had left the room. I caught up with her at the desk; she was printing the emails and the list. She handed me copies of each and dropped into her chair. I sat and started to read.

The first was short, but it was a bombshell.

SEAN, *Darling, let's not let this thing get out of hand. I have made up my mind. You are the man for me and I do not plan to let you go. You know what I am like when I make up my mind . .*

Sonia

THE SENDER'S name and email address were at the foot: Sonia Vincenzo. Dehan whistled. I looked up. We stared at each other.

"You thought it was interesting because of his haircut? Stone, this case is Pandora's box. What's next? Love letters from the White House?"

I closed my eyes and shook my head. "Sean O'Conor in bed—literally, not figuratively—with the capo of the New Jersey Mob's only niece? That is a serious plot twist."

She was scanning the next sheet. She said, "Keep reading."

I flipped it over and read:

LISTEN, *you sad piece of shit, if you think you can climb in these pants and then just walk away with a kiss and a wink, think again! Your Irish fucking charm don't cut no ice with me or with my uncle. I hope you got your knees insured, Sean, because you are going to need all the fucking medical attention you can get when Dino and his pals get through with you, you fucking Mick bastard. You are dead!*

"HELL HATH no fury like a woman scorned. If that's how she felt about Sean, how do you think she felt about Alicia?"

I spread the third sheet on my desk and looked at it. It was just a short list of names.

PADRAIG O'NEIL
  Sadiq Khan
  Robert Bellini

DEHAN DROPPED the paper on the desk.

"Who is Robert Bellini?"

I shook my head. "I have no idea."

"Sonia Vincenzo is an attorney, isn't she?"

"Yeah. And she works for her uncle. Talking to her is going to be about as useful as talking to the wall." I gazed out at the gathering dusk. "Unless . . ."

Dehan spoke my thoughts, "Unless you can lure her into trying to incriminate Sean." I nodded and she went on. "Sean is dead, but the legend of the saint lives on, and once the press gets hold of this, he will become a martyr. However, if she can be induced to talk, his memory might be ruined forever."

"Yup, and once she starts talking, maybe I can catch her in a lie. It's worth a try. I don't want you to come along."

She raised an eyebrow at me. "Any reason?"

"Yup. She'll open up to a man; the minute you give her a taste of your attitude, she'll clam up."

She grinned. "Fair point. What do you want me to do?"

"I want a name for every single one of those kids in that photograph, and I want to know what happened to them and where they are today. If we are going to get any real evidence, it will be from them. Talk to the captain, see if he'll allocate us some help tracing those kids."

She nodded and went upstairs. I found Sonia Vincenzo's firm, called, and made an appointment for the following morning at ten. I was yawning and stretching when Dehan came back down. She looked drawn and tired. I realized she'd been about thirty-six hours without sleep. I got to my feet.

"Come on, kiddo, that's enough for one day. I'm taking you home."

She stood nodding, lots, like she really agreed with me, but gazing at the floor like she couldn't make up her mind about something.

"I left my car at your place."

"You okay to drive?"

"Yeah, I'm fine, but let me stop off at a supermarket on the way. Okay?"

"Sure."

We stopped at Kmart on Bruckner Boulevard. She jumped out and said, "Two minutes!" as she slammed the door. She ran across the parking lot and I smiled at how long her legs were. Not many women could get away with legs that long and slim, but she had all the elegance and grace supermodels pretended to have. Only with Dehan, it was real.

I frowned at myself and changed my train of thought. I thought about Sean and Conor, and Father O'Neil, the photographs, and now Sonia Vincenzo. It was like having a jigsaw puzzle with too many pieces. The picture was already pretty much complete, so what the hell do you do with the extra pieces? I drummed on the wheel. Granted, there were uncomfortable questions, but how did the photographs, and the niece of the New Jersey capo, explain Sean being dressed as a tramp, and Alicia's disappearance?

I rubbed my face with my palms and told myself, enough. Dehan was walking back toward the car with a paper bag. She had a nice swing to her hips and she was smiling. She climbed in the car and slammed the door.

"Okay, let's go."

I looked at the bag as I turned the key. There was a bottle of wine poking out and a few other bits and pieces. I smiled and pulled away.

"You got a date?"

She laughed a bit too loud. "Yeah. This guy I've been seeing."

I was surprised. "Really? Is it serious?"

She stared out the side window. "You kidding? It's like we're married."

I pulled onto the Boulevard. "Wow! That good, huh? How come you didn't tell me?"

She looked at me a moment with an odd expression.

"I didn't say it was good. I said it was like we were married."

I laughed and said no more, wondering why I felt suddenly tired and irritable instead of just tired.

I pulled in behind her car and we both climbed out. She stood staring at me over the roof as I locked the Jag. She spoke suddenly. "What are you having for dinner?"

I raised my eyebrows and made a "Pffff!" noise. "I hadn't thought about it really. Cheese on toast?"

She held up the bag and smiled. It was an odd expression, timid, apologetic, hopeful, almost pleading. "I got sirloin. I also got bacon, and eggs, to replace the stuff I keep eating."

She caught me off guard and I didn't know what to say. After a moment, I laughed. "Sure! That's great! You didn't have to, but I'm glad you did."

She didn't move, just stood staring at me. "You sure you don't mind?"

"Yeah! Of course I don't. Come on, let's go inside." I took a step, but she didn't move. "Carmen, are you okay?"

"Stone?"

"Yeah?"

The pale amber glow from the streetlamp was touching her

face in the growing darkness. I saw the wet gleam of a tear on her cheek. She looked scared.

"I need to talk to you."

"What about, Carmen?"

"Promise me . . ."

I took a step toward her. "Promise you what, Dehan?"

"Promise me you'll keep me as your partner. Promise me you won't dump me or request a transfer."

"What are you talking about?"

"Promise me!"

"Of course I won't, Dehan! What's this about?"

"I am going to tell you the truth . . . the truth about me."

TEN

A SOFT BREEZE MOVED HER HAIR ACROSS HER FACE. IT seemed to be the only movement in the world at that moment. I nodded once, said, "Okay," and turned and walked to the door. I opened it and went in, leaving it open behind me. I switched on the kitchen light, proceeding to turn on the living room lamps and pull the drapes. I heard the door close behind me.

She was in the kitchen, putting her bag down on the side. She took a plate from the draining board and dropped the steaks on it, still wrapped in paper. I approached the breakfast bar and stood watching her a moment unpacking the bag and opening the wine. She spoke without looking at me.

"Young Jewish man has been shot, he's bleeding to death. He manages to stagger home to his parents' house, where he rings the bell and falls to his knees. His mother opens the door and he says to her, 'Mamma, I'm dying!' She puts her hands on her hips and says, 'You'll die, but foist you'll eat!'"

I smiled. "You told me that one already, but you told me it was your aunt."

She shrugged. She still wouldn't look at me. "It might have been. Kind of thing she would have said." I drew breath and she raised a finger. "Don't ask. I'll tell you in my own time."

"I was going to say I could peel some potatoes."

She nodded. The cork popped and she poured two glasses. "It needs to breathe. I got a good one."

I pulled a bag of potatoes from the vegetable trolley. "You hungry?" I wasn't.

I was too tired to be hungry, but Dehan said, "Starving."

I chose four big ones and started peeling. She started making a large salad.

"That's what my dad was like: 'You'll die, but foist you'll eat.' He was gentle, the true meaning of a gentleman. He was generous, and kind. But he was strong, what we call a mensch. And his family was everything to him."

I smiled at the potato as I cut it into strips. "Were you a daddy's girl?"

"You bet. When does a stereotype become an archetype, Stone?"

"I don't know. I never thought about it."

"It was the kind of question my dad was always asking. And he had an answer for all of them. A stereotype is always consistent. An archetype is full of contradictions." She took the chopped potatoes and dropped them into the oil. They hissed loudly. "He was talking about himself." She imitated his voice, "'If I had been a stereotypic Jew, I would not have married your mother. But as a Jewish archetype, I had to marry your mother!'"

I smiled again. "An intelligent man."

"Part of the archetype."

I nodded. "I guess."

She was quiet for a while, watching the potatoes fry. She said suddenly, "Why is north up? Why are the French rude? Why does the Earth wobble? Why are Africans black? You name it, he asked it, and had an answer. It was like he was trying to get inside the mind of God, and explain it."

She tested one of the French fries. Then she put the griddle on to heat with a bit of oil and sprinkled coarse salt over the meat.

When the griddle was smoking, she threw the steaks on. They hissed and flames leapt up around them.

"But there are no answers, Stone, no explanations. All you can do is describe, you can't explain."

"Isn't that a little fatalistic, Carmen?"

She shrugged and flipped the steaks. "Maybe. You want to put the fries on the plates?"

We sat and ate in silence for a while. The steaks were good, so was the wine. After a bit, she said, "The fifteenth of January, 2005, was a Saturday."

I sat back. Sean O'Conor's body had been found on the Sunday morning, on the sixteenth.

"Mom and Dad had closed the café. We'd had dinner, and I was eighteen. They had rented a movie, *Harry Potter and the Prisoner of Azkaban*. My dad loved that kind of thing, he was such a dreamer. Mom said she loved it, but we knew that after ten minutes she'd go make a cup of tea, start washing up, clean the windows . . ." She smiled, focused on my face, then my plate. "You're not eating."

She sipped. I couldn't eat, but I forced myself. I cut a slice of meat and stuffed it in my mouth.

"It was nine o'clock. We heard hammering on the door. My dad went down to see who it was. We heard voices, my dad trying to reason with somebody. The other voice was . . ." She was searching for the word. "Sneering, contemptuous, amused, overpowering. It scared me. Then we heard feet on the stairs."

"Who was it?"

She cut savagely into her steak. "I should tell you first that for a few weeks he had been coming on to my mom. He didn't like me; I was 'too Jewish,' but my mom was real pretty, even at forty she was trim and cute. She went to see Father O'Neil for advice because she didn't know what to do. My dad was strong, in his mind and in his personality, but physically he didn't stand a chance."

"Against who, Dehan?"

"So Father O'Neil tells her . . ." She laughed a dry, sick laugh. "He tells her to pray, this was his guidance. From a church that sacked the wealth of the Western world, that marched to war against the most powerful warriors and empires in history, his advice is, accept the fate that God has decreed for you, and don't forget to pray. Pray for forgiveness. And now the time had come, there in our living room, with the TV on, and my father standing there shaking, and I felt so sick I was going to throw up right there on the floor. He was there, drunk, stinking of whiskey, to claim what he said was his."

"Father O'Neil?"

"Mick Harragan."

I went cold. "Mick."

"He raped her. My dad tried to stop him, but Mick beat him to a pulp. He put him in the hospital, and he beat me up too, until I couldn't move. Then he raped her, right there in front of us. He told us that if we talked, we would all watch each other die, and if he didn't do it, the Sureños would, or the Jersey Mob."

I searched for words, but it was like she had said, there were no answers, no explanations. There was nothing I or anybody else could say. I watched her attack her steak with a kind of controlled fury. She chewed, swallowed, sipped her wine.

"He was in hospital for six weeks. He didn't want to come home. Every time he looked at Mom, his heart was filled with shame and humiliation. Her heart was broken. She had been violated, and her husband, her man, and her daughter had watched it happen. Mick Harragan had not only destroyed them physically, he had broken their souls and destroyed our family. On the twelfth of June, 2005, my dad died. Three weeks later, my mom died. I promised them, I literally swore on their graves, nobody would ever do that to me. Nobody would ever break me or take my soul."

I sat staring at the half-eaten steak on my plate. My mind was racing, trying to get a grip on all the implications, on what it meant. I said, "Kirk?"

"Downstairs, in the car, keeping watch."

"That's why you knew where he lived."

"I'd been hunting for Harragan for a long time."

"They are dead now, Dehan, both of them."

She smiled. "Yeah, I was robbed of that right, but I guess Maria Garcia had earned it."

"It's over."

"Is it?"

"You have to let it go."

"You promised . . ."

"I am not going to dump you! We're partners. We are more than partners. Hell . . . !" I gestured at the table, the food, and the wine. "But for your own sake, you need to let go. They are dead!"

"On Saturday, the fifteenth of January, 2005, Sean O'Conor was executed, dressed as a tramp, and thrown in a dumpster on Lafayette. Just around the corner, just down the road from my parents' house, Alicia vanishes on the same night. And on that same night, Mick Harragan comes to my parents' house and rapes and murders my family. Do you think that is all coincidental?"

"No."

She reached in her pocket and pulled out some folded A4 papers. As she opened them, I saw they were the emails and the list. She turned to the last page and put it in front of me.

Padraig O'Neil
 Sadiq Khan
 Robert Bellini

"Do you remember what Father O'Neil said to us just before he left?" I nodded. She went on, "Because I have it branded on my memory, verbatim: '. . . What when it is the police doing the murdering and the raping? Who do you call then?' He was talking about Harragan, and you know it."

She was right.

"Harragan is dead, Dehan. So is Kirk."

She held my eye a long time. Finally, she said, "So are my mom and my dad, and my cousin Alicia, and so probably are those twelve girls in the photo." She put her finger on the list. "But Father Padraig O'Neil, Sadiq Khan, Robert Bellini, and 'H' are not."

ELEVEN

She stayed the night in the guest room. I didn't sleep well, and by six I had showered and gone down to make coffee. I found her sitting at the kitchen table staring into a cup of coffee.

"It's hot. I heard you and made a fresh pot."

I poured myself a cup and rested my ass against the sink. "No bacon this morning. What's wrong, you don't love me anymore?"

She didn't smile, but seemed to study me for a minute.

"Do I need to regret telling you what I told you last night?" I shook my head and drew breath to answer, but she interrupted me. "Don't give me a clever, evasive answer, Stone. Be straight with me."

"Have I ever been anything else?"

"No."

"I'm not about to start. You don't need to regret it. I'm not going to ask for you to be transferred, or for a different partner. I like working with you. But I am going to make something real clear, so there is no mistake and no confusion. We are cops, we are not vigilantes, and it is our job to catch suspects, not punish bad guys." She just kept watching me. She didn't answer or react. "I am trusting you, Dehan. Don't betray my trust. Don't put me in a position of having to choose."

"I won't."

She stood and started making breakfast. I heard the hiss of the bacon in the pan, and smelled the rich aroma on the air.

"But you're wrong about one thing, Stone." She said it as she was cutting bread and putting it in the toaster. "We are not vigilantes, that's true, but we are not cops either." She turned to face me. "We are people, hot-blooded, living people."

ROBERTS AND LEVINE, the firm Sonia worked for, was on First Avenue, near the corner with East 64th. It occupied the two top floors of an unassuming red brick that was only four stories high. But the inside left you in no doubt about what league they were in. The reception was small and cozy, and all the available wall space was taken with photographs of Roberts and Levine's senior partners drinking champagne with various presidents and film stars, as well as the heads of the main Manhattan "Families."

The receptionist cocked her head on one side and smiled in a way you just knew she practiced in front of the mirror at home, and said, "She's in a meeting right now, but said you should go right on up anyway."

I frowned. "She's in a meeting, but she wants me to go up?"

"That's what she said."

I took the elevator to the third floor. There were just two offices and a girl sitting at a desk. She gave me the same smile as the girl downstairs. Maybe they practiced together. I told her who I was and she pointed at a door. "They're expecting you. Just go right on in."

"They?"

She smiled. I went in.

It was a corner office, the size of an average apartment. It was decorated with old-world elegance. The walls were lined with books. Some of them even looked as though they were used sometimes. Her desk was large and made of oak. She was sitting behind it, and her uncle, Don Alvaro Vincenzo, was sitting on the corner of it. Over to the left, there was a sofa with two chairs and a coffee table. There was a man sitting there on the sofa, who looked as though he could break bricks with his face. All three of them were watching me.

I smiled sweetly and closed the door. "Good morning, which one of you is Sonia Vincenzo?"

The guy with the dangerous face glanced over at Sonia and her uncle with a "well, it's not me, so it must be one of you guys" expression.

Alvaro said, "I like a man with a sense of humor, Detective Stone, it's a shame you haven't got one." Then he laughed out loud, staring with manic eyes, first at his hard man and then at his niece.

Sonia said, "Come in, Detective. I hope you don't mind, I have asked Don Alvaro and Mr. Vitale to join us."

She was beautiful. She looked like she'd been made by Armani: today she was exquisite, tomorrow she'd be out of fashion, and by next year, her seams would be coming undone. I shook my head.

"I don't mind at all. I am just wondering why."

She indicated a chair across from her desk and I sat. Don Alvaro smiled down at me. He was a tall, elegant man with expensive, gray hair and an expensive suit.

"We don't often talk to the cops these days, Detective Stone, usually it's the Feds." He said it with urbane humor, like he thought he was being sophisticated.

Sonia said, "It pays to take precautions. With all the microtechnology that you boys use now, it is good to have some reliable witnesses to contextualize the stuff you record. It would not be the first time the NYPD have tried to entrap a member of my family."

I grinned. "Yes, I have often wondered why we target the

Vincenzo family, such decent, upstanding members of the community." I turned to Alvaro. "How is Pro, by the way?"

His smile wasn't so much thin as anorexic. "What do you want, Stone?"

I turned back to Sonia. "Actually, I have no interest in your family at all, Ms. Vincenzo. I wanted to ask you about somebody else."

Her eyes narrowed. "Who?"

"Sean O'Conor."

If I had slapped her in the face with a wet mullet she wouldn't have looked more surprised. I glanced at Don Alvaro. His face was like granite, but he had two cute pink spots on his cheeks. Sonia shrugged.

"Sean . . . Why, I have had no contact with Sean for over ten years."

The Don slid his ass off the desk and walked over to stare out the window.

"What was the nature of your relationship, Ms. Vincenzo?"

"Relationship . . . ? I wouldn't describe it as a relationship . . . We were acquaintances . . ."

"Acquaintances. How did you meet?"

"We met at law school. We were both working in Manhattan. We met occasionally for a drink . . ."

I studied her face a minute, still smiling. "If you'll forgive me saying so, you seem . . ." I spread my hands. "Odd bedfellows, metaphorically speaking, of course."

She frowned. "What do you mean?"

"Him, a devout Catholic, champion of the poor and the needy, savior of souls; you, a member of the . . ." I smiled at Don Alvaro's back. He was rigid. ". . . immensely powerful Vincenzo empire."

He turned to raise an eyebrow at me. She said, "We were just acquaintances, Detective."

"Not bedfellows? Do you happen to know where he is now?"

"We lost touch."

"Did you correspond?"

"Correspond?"

"By email, for example. Did you ever exchange emails?"

She could sense a trap. So could her uncle, and he was watching her like a hawk.

"We may have exchanged a few."

I let her see in my eyes that I knew that. What I wasn't sure about yet was whether her uncle knew that. I took a slightly different tack.

"What kind of man was he, Ms. Vincenzo?"

"Well." She shrugged. "I didn't know him that well . . ."

"Really?" I waited, giving her space. She glanced at her uncle but didn't say anything, and so I moved in. "Because I was under the impression that you two were pretty close."

"I don't know what could have . . ."

"Didn't you, for example, write to him threatening to put him in hospital if he broke up with you?"

I felt rather than heard the tough guy stand up. Alvaro gave him a "hang on" look. Nobody spoke for a moment.

"I don't know what the source of your information is, Detective."

I put a smile on the right side of my face.

"Cute, a lawyer's answer. But you and I both know what the source of my information is. You wrote that email, and clearly, if I have read it, it must still exist." I looked up at the Don. "Did you know about their relationship, Don Alvaro?"

He didn't answer; he just gave me the dead eye.

"See, the thing is, Sonia, that right after you wrote him that email, he was executed." I looked back at Don Alvaro. "And I do mean, executed."

She looked shaken. "I didn't even know he was dead."

"What, didn't you ask your uncle not to tell you when it was done?"

She sighed. "I'm an Italian, Detective Stone, we are hot-blooded and passionate. When we fight, we say things in the heat of the moment, but we don't mean them. It's bluster. It doesn't mean anything. Sean and I were having an affair. I wanted to make it more permanent. He was . . . He was a very special kind of man. He told me he couldn't live with me. He believed the stories about my family, and me. So he told me he was breaking it off. I was hurt; my pride was hurt, so I wrote him a very foolish email. That was all there was to it."

"And within the week he turns up dead."

"That had nothing to do with me."

I made a skeptical face and gave my head a little shake. "I just keep wondering, keep turning it over in my mind, how does a guy like Sean, as pure as the driven snow, wind up being killed in a textbook Mob execution?"

"I don't know."

"Because right now, Sonia, your email comes damn close to being a confession." I looked at her uncle. He had a face that could have sent a zombie back to its grave. "I think you had better explain, Don Alvaro, that this is a time to be cooperative, because two things are about to happen. First, I am this close"—I held up my thumb and my index finger to show how close I was—"to pulling you both in on a charge of murder one."

Alvaro said, "You're bluffing," but he wasn't sure.

"And two, Sean's murder is about to hit the news. He is not only going to become a national hero, an Irish Catholic battling organized crime single-handed, he is also going to become a martyr in the local, Catholic communities that you prey on. He's going to be the guy who stood up against the Irish Mob and the Mafia to fight for the little guy, the homeless children and the exploited mothers, and was ruthlessly murdered for it, by you. And I am wondering, how is it going to look when Don Alvaro Vincenzo's niece is implicated, and her email, threatening to have him murdered, is leaked to the press? If I were you, I'd be thinking about avoiding that ever happening. And your best way of doing that right now is to tell me everything you know about Sean O'Conor."

I sensed King Kong sit down behind me. The tension eased, and Don Alvaro looked at Sonia. "So?"

She studied my face for a long time. You could almost hear the cogs turning in her head. Finally, she shook her head. "So nothing. There is nothing more to tell. I was young, he was an exceptional man. I guess I thought he could offer me a way out of this." She looked up at her uncle. "An escape from *la cosa nostra*. We fucked a few times. For him it was some kind of release, a moment of madness, for me it was hope. It was never going to last."

"That's very touching and insightful. Did he ever share information with you about what he was involved in?"

She sighed, hesitated. "If I were smart, Stone, this is where I would tell you that he was corrupt, trying to blackmail my family, secretly taking payoffs from the Irish, and that's why he got hit. But I am not going to do that. Aside from screwing me, he was everything he appeared to be." She thought a moment. "Was I mad enough to have him killed? Yeah, I was. Did I think about it? Yes, I did. Did I do it? No. No, because my dad and my uncle would have been furious with me for getting involved in the first place, and because bottom line was, I still loved him."

I repeated, "What was he involved in?"

"As far as I know, he was going up against the Hagan clan. Something to do with squatters."

"Anything else?"

She frowned. "There was something. He was real vague about it. He said it was going to send shock waves through the Catholic establishment, but he never told me what it was."

I looked up at Don Alvaro. His face was about as expressive as a frozen Swede who'd died of boredom waiting for a bus.

"How'd you feel about shock waves in the Catholic establishment, Alvaro?"

"I don't give a fuck what the Irish do. Who gives a fuck about the fucking Micks?"

I turned back to Sonia. "What about other women?"

"Sean?" She sounded incredulous, giving a little laugh. "I don't think so."

I stood. "You don't need an Irish saint to come and save you, Sonia. You just need enough backbone to keep you upright while you walk away." I glanced at Don Alvaro. "Say hi to Pro for me."

He didn't answer.

TWELVE

I picked Dehan up outside the precinct and we headed for East 161st Street to meet Conor Hagan. His construction company had the top floor on a 1930s redbrick office block on the corner of Park Avenue. We arrived punctually at five to twelve. We told the pretty receptionist who we were. She listened with interest, cocked her head on one side, and smiled. Maybe they taught them to do that in Receptionist School.

"He's not here? He went out to lunch? But he said to tell you where he was if you wanted to join him."

I smiled back. "Good. Tell me."

"He's at the Shamrock? Two blocks down, on Melrose Avenue?"

I frowned. "Are you telling me or asking me?"

She frowned back.

Dehan said, "She's telling you. Come on."

In the elevator, I said, "We'll get in the car now? We'll drive to the Shamrock? Talk to Conor Hagan?"

"You're a real ass, you know that?"

"You're, like, hurting my feelings?"

"Stop it or I will hurt you. And not just your feelings."

Conor Hagan was hard to miss. He was six four and looked like Michelangelo's less talented cousin had made him out of concrete. He was sitting at a table in the corner with a pint of Guinness and a couple of beef sandwiches. There was a sheaf of papers in front of him and he was absorbed in reading them. He looked up as we approached. He ignored our badges and studied our faces as I told him who we were.

He indicated the chairs opposite and put his papers away in a briefcase by his side. As we sat, he said, "What do you want?"

His accent was Bronx, with overtones of Dublin.

"We'd like to talk to you about Sean O'Conor."

"Who?"

Dehan said, "Sean O'Conor, he . . ."

"That's like saying to an Englishman, I want to talk to you about John Smith, or to an Indian, I want to talk to you about Arjun Patel. I must know at least a hundred Sean O'Conors. Who the fuck is Sean O'Conor?"

His eyes were pale blue and hard. They were the eyes of a killer, ruthless and dispassionate.

Dehan sighed. "Out of the hundreds of Sean O'Conors that you know, how many of them have tried to block a building project while protecting the rights of the squatters who were inhabiting the building you wanted to develop?"

He bit into his sandwich and chewed. "You're talking about Tiffany Street." It wasn't a question, so I didn't answer. "2004. Sean O'Conor. He was the piece of shit who organized it, from his shabby little offices on Sheridan Avenue. What about him?"

"When was the last time you saw him?"

"I never saw him. He talked to my lawyers. My lawyers tried to talk to him."

She persisted. "What did your lawyers think? Did he have a case?"

His eyes were not just hard, they were aggressive, seemingly tearing her apart to see what was going on inside.

"No."

"Why not? He said he had proof your agents had accepted rent."

"Some of them had, without my knowledge, and they were dealt with. But before he ever came along with his little crusade, I had already made arrangements with the church to have them rehoused, and those that couldn't be rehoused, given shelter. The building was unsafe and unfit for human habitation, and there were kids in there that were not being schooled. Some were orphans. There were mothers out of their fucking minds on crack; some of the fucking kids were addicted. I wanted them out and on some kind of program to get them rehoused and the kids into school. The government was less than fucking cooperative, so I talked to the church, offered them money, and we made a deal. So Sean fucking O'Conor had no case from the word fucking go."

I frowned and scratched my chin. "You got proof of this?"

He leaned forward and stared hard into my eyes. "I don't need fucking proof. You got a problem with me, it's up to you to adduce proof. Isn't it, copper?"

"I haven't got a problem with you, Conor. I'm just trying to understand what went down. Have you got proof?"

"Of course I've got fucking proof. The whole thing was drawn up with lawyers and contracts."

"And Sean knew this?"

"He should have. He was told often enough, and I had my lawyers take him the fucking documents to see. But he wouldn't have it, so fucking stupid. Nothing would do for him but that the work was stopped and there be a fucking inquiry into the conditions in which those people were living."

"Did you ever talk to him?"

He thought about it and nodded. "Yeah, in January, just after Christmas. I phoned him and told him to leave the fucking case alone, he didn't stand a chance. I told him if he didn't drop it I'd fucking bury him and he'd never practice again in New York."

"What did he say?"

"He was babbling some shite about how he was going to

expose me for the scum I was." He sat back and his face sank into shadows. "Anyway, I must have got through to him because he dropped the case and nothing more was ever heard of him. Why all the questions?"

Dehan said, "He was murdered."

He leaned forward and raised an eyebrow. "Good, but my beef with him was twelve years ago. If I had been planning on killing him, I would have done it back then. Plus, I would have enjoyed the whole fucking court case farrago because I would have shown the miserable twat up for the fucking gobshite he was."

There was a trace of a smile on her face. She gave it a beat, then said, "He was executed twelve years ago, on the fifteenth of January, just after you spoke to him and told him you would bury him. And his body was found in one of your dumpsters, on Lafayette, just by Father O'Neil's church."

He was quiet for a long time, staring at his Guinness. He didn't look scared or worried, he was just thinking, calculating. Finally, his brow contracted and his eyes narrowed. He looked up at Dehan. "The tramp. That tramp was Sean O'Conor."

I raised my own eyebrow. "You've got a good memory."

"No. I have a superb memory. And I'm not a thick, fucking Mick, so don't think you can pull one over on me or stick me in the frame." He pointed a finger like a beef sausage at me. "Come after me, Stone, and I will destroy you both. Make no fucking mistake."

I gave him a look of boredom. "Bring it down a level or two, Conor. Nobody is coming after you, and you are not going to destroy me. If it wasn't you who had Sean executed that night, who was it?"

"I don't know."

Dehan said, "Whoever it was, was operating on your patch."

"I know."

"So you must have some idea who it was. Was it the Italians?"

His face was sour. "I told you, I don't know. Get out. I'm sick of looking at your fucking faces. You spoiled my lunch, just fuck off out of here."

I said, "I'm not done yet. What about Father O'Neil?"

He picked up his Guinness and drained half of it. He wiped his mouth on the back of his hand.

"What about him?"

"How well do you know him?"

"Very well."

"What's your opinion of him?"

"He's a gobshite. He wishes he was Mother Teresa but he hasn't got the balls. Now have you got any more stupid questions for me? 'Cause I'm losing my patience."

Dehan smiled. "What happens if you lose your patience, Conor?"

"I call the cops and have youse removed."

Outside, we walked slowly toward the car. Spring was still trying to make things look beautiful, but it wasn't doing a great job.

I looked up at the sky. It was very blue. "What do you make of him?"

"A showman. Underneath that noisy exterior, he's a ruthless businessman. Whatever he says about how he would have enjoyed the trial, he did the numbers and saw it would be cheaper and more expedient to have Sean killed. He killed him."

"Makes sense."

She watched her feet as she walked for a bit. "He got upset when I told him the tramp had been identified as Sean."

I nodded. "He did. That's when he told us to leave."

We came to the car and I sat on the trunk. I could see my face distorted in the lenses of her aviator shades. "The way it looks right now, Sean was threatening to expose a child prostitution ring run by Conor Hagan, with the possible collusion of Father O'Neil and three other people . . ."

She was shaking her head. "Run by Conor Hagan and Mick

Harragan, with the possible collusion of Father O'Neil and two other people."

"Okay, Conor warned him off, he wouldn't listen, so he and Alicia were murdered."

She nodded.

"Now, we have a problem, Dehan. The only piece of physical evidence we have points to a completely different person, and a completely different motive. Sonia Vincenzo, the jilted lover, and her rage and jealousy."

I had told her about my meeting with Sonia on the way in the car. She sighed and thrust her hands into her pockets. "You don't buy that, do you?"

"Right now I'm not buying anything but lunch. But the fact stands that that is our only piece of evidence."

She nodded. "The captain gave us two uniforms to help with tracking those kids, Stevens and Ortega. Let's see if we've had any hits."

THIRTEEN

WHILE I WAS TALKING TO SONIA VINCENZO, DEHAN had got a complete list from the parish archive of the twelve girls who had been in Alicia's class in January of 2005. Of the twelve, three had no national insurance number. Those three, and four others, were either orphans or presumed orphans, in that nobody knew where their parents were. Of the confirmed orphans, none of them had ever known their father, in four cases the mother had died of an overdose, and John had murdered one. In all cases—all twelve—the mothers were prostitutes. The five girls who were not orphans were theoretically in foster care, but three had escaped to go on the game and two had been kicked out for their violent behavior, and nobody had bothered to inform the agency or the court.

Dehan had got a large whiteboard and put it by the desk. Then she'd cropped the photographs so you could only see the face and taped them on the board, with their names written by the picture.

When we got back, that was all that was written by any of the pictures, and Stevens and Ortega were packing up to leave the station. Stevens saw us approaching the desk and stood.

"Detectives, we have had consistently negative results on all the names and the NI numbers. The parish record lists the course as closing down on the twenty-first of January, 2005. That is the last official record that we can find of those children. We have checked state and federal databases, hospitals, FBI . . ." He shook his head and shrugged. Ortega rose and joined us, nodding his confirmation of what Stevens was saying. "There is just no record of any of these kids. They haven't acquired driving licenses, they have no credit cards, they haven't been sick, got married, died . . ."

Ortega shrugged with his eyebrows. "Not officially, anyway. So we were on our way to the neighborhood to canvass the homes around there, see if anybody remembers them."

I nodded. "Good, good work."

They left. We followed. Sometimes—often—that's what detective work is, walking door-to-door, ringing on doorbells, stopping people in the street, and that's what we did. We put up flyers, we handed out photographs, we knocked on doors, and visited community centers.

In the Bronx, the cops are not everybody's favorite people. So canvassing is often not a productive method of investigation. You tend to get blank stares, shrugs, and shaking heads. But when missing kids are involved, it's different, especially with the women. We found plenty in the neighborhood of Tiffany Street and Lafayette who remembered one or more of the kids. Nobody knew where they were now, and nobody, not a single person, remembered seeing them after January 2005.

By half past seven, we gave it up and went back to the precinct. Stevens and Ortega came in shortly after us, reporting the same result. The kids were known. The kids were remembered, but nobody had seen them since those pictures were taken. I thanked them for their help and turned to Dehan.

"Let's go see the captain."

We climbed the stairs and knocked on his door.

"Come!"

We went in and he smiled broadly, like he thought we were amusing.

"Ah, Stone and Dehan, the Dynamic Duo, what can I do for you? Please, sit!"

We sat and I laid out the case for him. He frowned and listened without interrupting. When I had finished, he said, "And they missed the haircut and the nails back in the original investigation?"

"Yes, sir. To be honest, I don't think there was an original investigation. There was no shell, no slug, no blood, no witness . . ." I shrugged. "Unsolved."

"So you have done well to get this far, but it is hard to see where you go from here."

Dehan stared at her boots. I could feel her aura crackling, but fortunately, the captain didn't have that kind of sensitivity. I coughed.

"Well, it seems to have progressed from a simple murder investigation, Captain, because we now seem to have also a child prostitution ring, and twelve missing girls."

"Yes, I see that. What do you propose to do?"

I stared at him a moment and sucked my teeth. When I spoke, even Dehan looked at me in surprise.

"I want to dig up the churchyard."

"You want to do what?"

"Where are those girls, sir?"

"But, Stone, you know I am always very supportive of you, but you can't just go marching in and dig up the grounds of a church!"

I nodded. "I know, sir, but the church was their last known location. It was also the last known location of Alicia Flores."

"Even so . . ."

"One skilled person may be able to disappear—vanish from all state and federal databases, if they were determined and put their mind to it. For twelve young girls, some as young as eleven years old, collectively to vanish is almost impossible, unless there was some concerted effort . . ."

Dehan added, "Or unless they were dead."

"And, sir, there is the same thinking behind both Sean and the girls."

He frowned. "What do you mean?"

"Sean was dressed as a tramp on the assumption that people don't give a damn about down-and-outs. They were right. If Captain Jennifer Cuevas had not decided to sideline me by giving me these cold cases, nobody would ever have investigated Sean's death. Nobody would even have known he was dead. And exactly the same is true of those girls. They were chosen because they were people nobody would ever care about. The same mind that killed Sean O'Conor, killed those girls."

He looked horrified. I felt Dehan frown hard at her boots. He said, "You cannot possibly be certain of that. You have no evidence other than theories and surmise!"

"That's why I need to dig up the churchyard."

"What makes you think these twelve girls are buried there?"

"Thirteen. Sean's fiancée." I sighed. "Think it through. Thirteen bodies. They are hard to dispose of. You can dump one in the river, maybe two. But thirteen?"

"I'm sorry, Stone. No judge is ever going to sign off on such slim evidence. I can see where you're coming from, and maybe you are right. But you need something a lot more convincing than just a theory."

I nodded. "I imagined as much, sir, but I thought I had better appraise you of where we are at in the investigation. Thank you. I'll keep you posted."

"Yes, do, please."

Dehan got to her feet with a rigid face. I opened the door for her, and as she went out, the captain said, "Stone?" He looked like his face was trapped in a slow wince.

I said, "Yes, sir?"

"Don't do anything . . . you know . . . crazy."

I looked surprised. "Of course not, sir!"

On the stairs going down, Dehan said, "So what are we going to do?"

I gave her the same surprised look I had given the captain. "Dig up the churchyard, of course."

"How are you going to do that?"

"I don't know yet. But if we are going to get evidence of Sean and Alicia's murder, and the murder of those girls, we have to find the bodies."

I stopped at my desk and grabbed my jacket. I stared down at the file on my desk with the photographs in it. I opened it and pulled out the list of names.

PADRAIG O'NEIL
Sadiq Khan
Robert Bellini

SHE CAME and stood close by my side. She ran her finger down the names.

"Even if you have a churchyard to bury them in, it takes some organizing to make fourteen people disappear from the face of the Earth."

I nodded. "Mick knew how to make friends in high places."

"You remember when we investigated the Nelson Hernandez murder, when we found Mick's body?"

"Mm-hm . . ."

"I always had the feeling that Pro and the Jersey Mob were being informed of what we were doing."

I nodded. "I had that feeling too. And it wasn't only Jennifer." I placed my finger next to hers on the last name on the list. She said, "'H.'"

I looked at her. "Yeah, 'H.'"

FOURTEEN

DEHAN STILL HAD HER CAR AT MY PLACE. WE DROVE IN silence through the gathering dusk as the lights started to come on in the city. Headlamps glowed, and shop fronts spilled amber onto the sidewalks, while everything that was not illuminated in some way turned gray and grainy. As we turned off Morris Park Avenue into Haight, she said, "Can I borrow your computer for five minutes?"

"Sure, what for?"

"It's just a gut feeling. Something nagging at the back of my mind."

I opened the door and switched on the lights. I pointed to the corner by the bow window where the computer sat on a small desk between the sofa and an armchair.

"Help yourself. You don't need to sign in."

She sat at the PC while I threw my jacket on the chair and went into the kitchen. I heard the Windows tune and said, "You want a drink?"

She was quiet for a moment and then spoke as she typed. "What you got?"

"Beer or whiskey."

She turned to look at me. She was smiling, a little surprised. "What are you going to have?"

"I need a whiskey, it's Irish. You want one?"

She turned back to the computer with a small laugh. "Yeah. Can't let you drink alone, right?"

I poured two generous measures, carried one to the computer, and sat on the sofa with the other. I pulled one of my occasional tables around, stretched out, and put my feet up. The first sip of amber fire eased my muscles and I sighed. I was aware Dehan was excited but figured she'd tell me why when she was ready. It didn't take long.

She switched off the PC and came and joined me on the sofa, sitting at the far end with her back against the armrest.

"Robert Bellini, born Roberto Bellini in Rome, Italy, is the bishop of the Diocese of St. Mary, which includes Lafayette and Father O'Neil's church."

I closed my eyes.

"Oh, Dehan, you just switched on the fan, lined up your cart-load of shit, and took your best shot, didn't you?"

I opened my eyes and looked at her.

She grinned. "I figure, if you're going to make a mess, may as well make a big one. Cheers, Big Ears."

I raised my glass and we drank.

I studied the whiskey in my glass for a bit, thinking about each of our suspects in turn. I spoke to my drink.

"Leaving aside the evidence for a moment, not that we have much to leave aside, but what we have, forget it for now. Does your gut tell you that Father O'Neil is capable of murdering fourteen people, twelve of whom are young girls and children?"

She sipped her drink and sat staring into the middle distance, holding the drink in her mouth. After a bit, she swallowed and said, "That is so hard to answer. So many killers don't look the part . . ."

"But that's not what I'm asking you, I am asking you what your gut tells you."

She shrugged and pulled a face. "My immediate reaction would have to be no. But it's like that quote, you know the one? 'All that is needed for evil to triumph is for good men to do nothing.'"

I curled my lip at my glass. "Edmund Burke. He never actually said it, but I get your point. Father O'Neil is the type to let sleeping dogs lie, and feeding dogs feast."

She seemed to sag suddenly. "Can I take my boots off?"

"That depends. Did you wash your feet this month?" I closed my eyes. "How about Hagan?"

"Funny." I heard her boots thud on the floor and felt her feet settle on the sofa beside me. "Does my gut think he could kill fourteen people? Yes, and fourteen hundred and fourteen thousand. That guy is a sociopath, he will do anything to achieve his ends."

"How about getting involved in child prostitution in the first place?"

She was quiet so long I opened my eyes and looked at her. She was staring at the carpet and chewing her lip. She met my gaze and shook her head. "My gut would say no."

"So Father O'Neil would get involved simply not to incur the wrath of the powerful, and Hagan would do the killing, but there is somebody missing who would act as a catalyst and actually make it happen in the first place. Somebody powerful enough to make Father O'Neil comply . . ."

"And to make Hagan do the killing . . ."

We stared at each other for a while. "Then there are Mick and Bishop Roberto Bellini, both of whom would have Father O'Neil dancing to their tune with no trouble. If we only had some physical evidence, something, to link one person to the girls or Sean."

She frowned. "Have you noticed how everybody in this case is Irish except the bishop . . ."

"And Sonia Vincenzo."

"They are both Italian."

She drained her glass, slid down to rest her head on the

armrest, and closed her eyes. "An alliance of Catholic mobs to run child pornography? It seems a little far-fetched."

I drained my glass too and closed my eyes. She was right, it did seem far-fetched; everything about this case seemed far-fetched. Mick Harragan's ghost rising from the shadows of the past, his rape of Dehan's mother, her sworn vengeance, honestly it all seemed a bit unreal. The twelve missing children, and Sean O'Conor dressed as a tramp, murdered, lying in a dumpster while his fiancée disappeared, along with the girls, all seemed excessive, like a nightmare that keeps getting darker and crazier. And in the background, in the shadows, the massive, wild form of Conor Hagan, lowering like some diabolical spawn from hell, and behind him, backlit by dancing red flames, the laughing form of the bishop.

I opened my eyes. There was gray light filtering in through the window. My right leg was numb because Dehan's socked feet were resting on it, cutting off the blood. Her eyes were closed and her mouth was open. She was snoring softly and still gripping her whiskey glass in her hands. My glass had fallen on the floor. I looked at my watch, it read six twenty.

I carefully eased myself out from under her feet and limped to the toilet. I washed and combed my hair, and when I got back down she was still asleep, though she had changed her position.

The phone rang while I was making coffee and bacon.

"Frank, good morning."

"Is it too early, Stone? Tell me to go to hell if it's too early, I have no sense of time."

"It's fine, Frank. I was up. I spent the night with a woman on the couch and had to get up because I had a cramp in my leg."

There was a long silence. "Really?"

"Yup."

"Wow . . ."

"Whatcha got, Frank?"

"Fingerprints on the photographs. They were very clear and well preserved, and the same prints were on every picture. Apart from your own, there are three sets. Thumbs on the front; index, middle, and ring on the back, as you would expect. By the size, they are men's."

"You run them through IAFIS?"

"Natch, ol' buddy, no matches. Whoever handled those pictures is not in the system."

"What about the comparison?"

"I was coming to that, it was a match. Who was it?"

"I'll tell you later, Frank, and thanks for rushing it. Remember to sleep. You got any rafters you can hang from there?"

"Anybody ever tell you you were funny? They lied."

I hung up. Dehan was sitting up, looking at me with sleeping eyes.

"We got prints?"

"Yup."

"That's good."

I nodded. "It's great. It's a breakthrough."

"Did we sleep on the sofa?"

"Don't worry. I still respect you."

"You're cooking! That's my job."

"Go upstairs and have a nice, hot shower. You'll feel better. I have something to tell you after."

FIFTEEN

When we arrived at St. Mary's, the mass was almost over. We sat at the back and listened to the end of the sermon. He had chosen Luke 18:16, suffer little children to come unto me. He had a good voice, compelling and strong, and it filled the church without the use of a microphone.

"And I ask you to meditate on this: What is the Lord telling us, when he says, suffer little children to come unto me? Is he telling us to be kind to little children? Is he telling us to be lenient and understanding with them? Is he telling us to provide for them, both physical and spiritual nourishment?

"Indeed he is. But he is telling us more than this. He is telling us that to achieve the Kingdom of Heaven, we must ourselves be as children. For only in that blessed state of innocence can we truly understand love, the love of Jesus Christ our Savior, and the sublime love and grace of God and the Holy Spirit. Only in that childlike state of sacred innocence can we find the divine echo of our holy state before the original sin, when we were fresh from God the Creator's hands.

"Therefore, teach your children, feed them, care for them and love them, for they carry the divine spark of our Father in their innocent hearts, but more than that, learn to be as they are. Let us all learn to be God's children in our hearts, for nothing is closer to God's heart, than a child . . ."

It went on like that for another five minutes, and shortly after that they all started filing out. Dehan and I made our way down the nave and found Father O'Neil descending from the altar. He looked a little startled.

"Detectives, I thought we had said everything to each other that we needed to say."

Dehan smiled like a woman who is scared to open her mouth because she is not sure what might come out.

I said, "I'm afraid not, Father. We need to talk to you some more about those photographs."

I said it loud enough to make him glance at the exiting congregation. He gestured at the door to the rectory.

I shook my head. "Actually, I would like to talk to you in the churchyard."

He looked a little sick. "In the churchyard? Whatever for?"

I didn't answer. After the last stragglers had departed through the great doors, we made our way through rolling echoes toward the vast wedge of light that lay across the stone floor at the entrance. He stood a moment, watching me. I passed him and led the way along the footpath around the back of the nave, where it was shielded from the road and the apartment block by dense, mature trees and made a closed angle with the old coach house.

I stopped among the fruit trees that stood there in the shelter of the old walls and studied his face. I saw anxiety there.

"Yesterday was not the first time you had seen those pictures, was it, Father?"

"This again?"

"Was it?"

"I already told you . . . !"

I interrupted him. "Father O'Neil, yesterday was not the first time you had seen those photographs, was it?"

His breathing was short, and I could see his hands were trembling.

"I had never before seen those photographs. You cannot . . . There is no way . . ."

"Your fingerprints are on them. You handled each and every one of them twelve years ago."

"That is an outright lie! There is no way fingerprints could last twelve years! You are trying to trick me into admitting something that is not true!"

Dehan was shaking her head. "A common mistake, Father. Fingerprints will last for years if they are protected. We have enough, right there, to arrest and convict you and put you away for the rest of your life, and believe me, Father, there is nothing I would rather do. Although, my partner thinks you can be useful to us, so he is in favor of cutting a deal with you."

His eyes were bulging and he was sweating. His voice shook when he spoke. "What kind of deal? I am admitting nothing, mind! But what kind of deal . . . ?"

I said, "I want to dig up the churchyard." I pointed to the small patch of fruit trees. "Right there."

His skin turned a pasty gray and his legs seemed about to fold. "Oh sweet Jesus."

I saw Dehan ball her fist and curl her lip. I put my hand on her shoulder. She stared at me. I shook my head. She looked back at Father O'Neil and snarled, "Suffer little children to come on to me? I ought to gut you right here and feed you to the dogs."

"What's it going to be, Father? We take you in and you take the fall, or you cooperate with us."

He did what he had to do, what he had always done, and yielded to the prevailing wind. He stared first at Dehan and then at me, with a crying face that made you want to slap him.

"I will cooperate, of course, but it's not what it looks like. It isn't what you think, you have to let me explain."

"Oh, believe me, I can't wait. We will have plenty of opportunity to talk in depth and in detail, but first, there are a couple of things I need to do. Number one, you are going to write me a letter of authorization, on letter-headed paper, with an official stamp, allowing me to dig up the whole damned churchyard if I need to. If you don't, I will get a court order from a judge. You understand me, Father O'Neil?"

He nodded. "Yes."

"Now you have one chance, one shot. I haven't decided what to do with you yet, but cooperate with me and I will listen to your story."

"I understand."

"After you have written the letter of authorization, I want a full confession, detailing the parts played by Mick Harragan, Conor Hagan, Sadiq Khan, Bishop Bellini . . ." I watched his face carefully as I mentioned each name, the frowns, and the winces. "All of them. Do we have a deal?"

He seemed to sway, like he was about to pass out. "Yes. Please, take me inside, I don't feel well."

"Okay." I took his arm. "Let's go."

We went to his study where he wrote out the letter of authorization in careful longhand, then signed and sealed it. After that, he called Mrs. Doyle and asked her to pack him an overnight bag.

"I shall be assisting the police with their inquiries over the next couple of days."

She looked impressed and hurried upstairs to prepare his bag.

At the station house, we left him in the care of a uniformed officer in one of the interrogation rooms and Dehan and I climbed the stairs to the captain's office. I knocked and opened the door as he answered. He looked surprised, but not as pleased as he had been the day before.

"Stone, Dehan. It seems like only yesterday . . ."

I dropped the letter on his desk and didn't sit down. He looked at it, then at us. He opened it and read it, then sighed.

"Detective Stone, you are an implacable man. I am glad I am on your side . . ." There was an implied "but," but he didn't go there. He dropped the letter on the desk and asked, "How did you secure this? Presumably if he is agreeable, there is nothing to dig up?"

It was Dehan who answered. "His fingerprints are on each and every one of the photographs, from twelve years ago."

He echoed the Father. "Sweet Jesus!"

I took back the letter. "He has agreed to cooperate fully on the condition we listen to his story, and on the off chance of a deal."

"There was no trickery or entrapment?"

"Of course not."

He rubbed his face with his hands. "The shit is really going to hit the fan, Stone. I don't want any of it to land on the Forty-Third, you understand me?"

I took a moment to answer. "The shit is going to land where the shit is going to land, Captain. We are cops simply doing our jobs, and if the investigating officers had done their jobs twelve years ago, we wouldn't be in this situation now."

Dehan had to speak up. She couldn't keep quiet.

"Sir, there are probably twelve or thirteen young girls' remains buried in St. Mary's churchyard. Those girls were probably forced into prostitution and murdered, and Father O'Neil has as much as admitted all of this. I am having trouble understanding exactly what the options are, and what it is we are discussing."

His face went rigid, but he couldn't think of an answer. I gave him a sweet smile and said, "Detective Dehan isn't looking to get promoted anytime soon, sir, but I would have to agree with her. We have no option but to dig."

He nodded. "Take four men, and a crime scene team. Where is Father O'Neil now?"

"In interview room three, waiting to give us a statement."

He frowned. "You can't hold him without charge. Once he has given you his statement, you either charge him or let him go."

I sighed. "Yes, sir."

He said, a little reluctantly, "It's good work, both of you."

"Thank you, sir."

As I opened the door, he said, "Stone, don't ambush me again. I'm on your side."

"Wasn't my intention, Captain, I just did what I needed to do to get the job done."

"And Dehan?"

"Yes, sir?"

"It was a fair point, it's just"—he spread his hands—"things aren't always that simple on this side of the desk."

"Yes, sir."

On the stairs, Dehan said, "You want me to take O'Neil's statement while you assemble the team and call Frank? I can join you at the church when we're done."

I stopped and stood chewing my lip for a minute. Then I shook my head.

"No, he's going to wriggle and writhe and squirm like a worm on a hook. He won't know whether to implicate the world and his cousin to save himself, or protect them all to save himself. We've got a few hours before we need to let him go. Let him sweat and think through all the angles. Sooner or later, he'll realize he's out of choices. Meanwhile, I want to see what we find under those trees before we talk to him."

"Makes sense to me."

SIXTEEN

FRANK'S TEAM HAD BROUGHT A BOBCAT IN THE BACK OF their truck, and before the guys with the shovels and spades could get started digging pits, the Bobcat had to uproot and remove the fruit trees. Meanwhile, I had the uniformed officers seal off the churchyard with tape. Once the trees had been pulled out and removed to one side, I had them set up screens, and the CSI team moved in. While the guys in uniform dug, the CSI team sifted. It was a slow and painstaking task, and it drew attention. Pretty soon there was a small crowd peering through the railings and standing behind the tape at the church gate, seeing if they could catch a glimpse of what was going on.

I saw Dehan looking at them.

"They were inevitable; we all knew some people would show up to watch."

"It will get back to Hagan pretty soon."

"And the bishop and Sadiq Khan, I'm counting on it." I looked at my watch. "We need to get back to Father O'Neil." I glanced at the shallow pits. There were no bones yet, but they had barely got started. "I'd hoped to have something to pressure him with, but we'll make the most of what we've got."

I called over to Frank where he was sifting through a pile of earth. "I'm going back to the station. Call me as soon as you find anything."

He didn't look up, but touched his forehead with two fingers in an affirmative salute.

My cell rang just as we were approaching the car. It was the precinct.

"Stone."

"Detective, it's John, the captain."

"Yes, Captain."

"Listen, Father O'Neil has gone."

"What?!"

"You left him too long, Stone. He got tired of waiting and he got spooked. He said he was leaving and there was nothing I could do to stop him. You hadn't charged him, and I couldn't arrest him without screwing up your investigation. You overplayed your damn hand, Stone!"

He was right and I knew it, and I swore accordingly.

"Did he say where he was going?"

"No, he just said he was leaving."

"Goddamn it!"

"Fix it, Stone. Now!"

He hung up. Dehan had stopped walking and was watching me. "He's gone."

"Gone?"

"He walked out. I tried to be too damned clever, Dehan. I should have charged him."

She shook her head. "If you had, he would have clammed up like an oyster."

"Where is he going to go?"

"To the bishop?"

I shook my head. "The bishop won't touch him with a barge pole."

"Hagan?"

"Too dangerous, none of his associates. Where the hell is he going to go?"

"Stone?" I looked at her, but I already knew what she was going to say. "His life is in danger, and right now he is all we've got."

"I know. Call in; get an APB put out to notify me if he's seen and then try calling his cell. I'm going to talk to Mrs. Doyle."

I found her in the kitchen making a beef stew. She looked pissed. She gave me a look that would have had Mikhail Bakunin standing to attention.

"Would yiz mind at all tellin' what in the name of Jaysus is goin' on? The Father gone and youse uprootin' me feckin' trees!"

"Mrs. Doyle, I need your help."

"It's not enough that you're causin' me all this feckin' hassle. I have to help you an' all!"

She picked up two handfuls of bloody meat in her hands and dumped them into a big, cast-iron pot. There was a loud hiss and clouds of steam billowed out.

"Father O'Neil has gone missing. He's in trouble, Mrs. Doyle, he could be in danger and we are trying to help him."

"Help him, indeed! Indeed! This is what youse call help, is it? A fine feckin' way to help a body, this is!"

She started peeling potatoes like she was auditioning for a slasher movie.

"You know who Conor Hagan is?"

"That bastard!"

"The Father may have got into trouble with Hagan . . ."

The ferocity of her peeling eased.

I pressed. "He was trying to help people and things got out of hand. He was helping us, giving us vital information, but he panicked . . ."

"He's a good man, but he never did have any balls."

"He walked out of the station and we don't know where he's gone."

She threw the potatoes in the pot and started axing some

carrots. She threw them in too and scowled at the contents of the pot like they didn't deserve her pity. "He wouldn't go to the bishop, dirty fecker. He might go to Father Sullivan, at St. Patrick's, or if he's got any sense, he'll come back here, to me."

"If he does . . ."

"You want me to call yiz."

"He needs protection."

"Don't you worry, I'll protect him!"

"Mrs. Doyle . . ."

"I'll call yiz, aye. Don't worry."

Dehan was waiting for me, sitting on the hood of my car. As I approached, she said, "His cell is switched off."

I opened the door.

"We'll try St. Patrick's."

St. Patrick's was at Clason Point, on Lacombe Avenue. It wasn't far, but the traffic was heavy, and it took us almost twenty minutes to get there via Bruckner Boulevard and Soundview Avenue. It was a quiet, residential suburb of detached houses with large gardens. I parked a hundred yards up the road by the junction with Thieriot and watched the church for five minutes. Nothing happened. Nobody went in or came out. No cars arrived.

"Let's go in and talk to Father Sullivan."

The road was really still and really quiet. The slam of the car doors was loud. There was a gentle breeze and the sound of birds in the maple trees. I felt uneasy, and though we started out at a steady walk, by the time we were approaching the church we had both broken into a steady jog.

It was a modest church, much smaller than St. Mary's. A simple nave with a small steeple and a bell tower. A broad flight of six steps led up to the porch, and I took them three at a time. We stepped inside. Like the street, it was still and quiet, though not completely silent. There was a murmur of voices that was interrupted by our footfalls.

Two men were standing by the north transept, talking softly

to a dark-haired man in a hassock. They looked at us standing in the doorway. We crossed ourselves and sat in the rear pews, like we were praying. The men left the priest and approached down the left aisle. They were both tall, sandy-haired and blue-eyed. They looked tough. They looked Irish.

They stepped out the door, and I could hear their feet on the steps outside and rose. The priest looked as though he was about to leave through a side door to the vestry. I raised my voice. "Father! Father Sullivan?"

He stopped and turned to face me.

"I am Father Sullivan."

We approached and showed him our badges. "Detectives Stone and Dehan. We are looking for Father O'Neil."

"And why are you looking here?"

Dehan smiled. "You don't seem surprised that two NYPD detectives should be looking for Father O'Neil."

He was younger than Father O'Neil, maybe in his late thirties or early forties. He returned Dehan's smile with the same lack of feeling that she had given it. "Presumably, you have your reasons. What I am curious about is why you think you might find him here."

"Whatever you are curious about, Father"—I gave him my own unfeeling smile—"we think he is here. Is he?"

"I haven't seen Father O'Neil for some time."

"You're a good Catholic, Father, you're working hard not to lie, but with every evasive answer you give us, you put Father O'Neil's life more at risk. Where is he?"

He narrowed his eyes at me. "His life is at risk?"

"I haven't got time to explain, Father Sullivan, but if he dies because of this delay, you will have to live with that on your conscience. Where is he?"

Somewhere in the distance, I heard the hum of a car engine. He heard it too. He shook his head. "I don't know."

The impulse to smack him was hard to resist. Dehan said, "You're a damn fool!"

I pointed at the exit. "Who were those men?"

He gave Dehan a once-over that had more disdain than regret and turned back to me. "They wouldn't tell me who they work for. They were also looking for Father O'Neil."

I took a step closer to him and stared him hard in the eye. "He is a key witness in a murder investigation. Those men may have been looking for him to silence him. If you don't help us find him, you could be sentencing him to death, Father Sullivan. You need to get with the program. Where was he going from here?"

He had the good grace to look a little ashamed and said, "He refused to tell me. I don't think he knew himself."

"You lend him your car?"

He nodded. I gave him my notebook and my pen. "License number, make, and model."

He wrote it down and I gave it to Dehan. "Get an APB put out, will you?" She walked away, dialing the precinct. I turned back to Father Sullivan. "If he comes back, keep him here and call me. If he contacts you, find out where he is and tell me. If you hear anything at all, I want to know."

He nodded.

The sun was sinking in the west and the shadows were growing long when I stepped out onto the stairs. Dehan was a couple of steps down, hanging up the phone. She looked up at me.

"White Ford Ka." She gave me the license number. "APB is out. What now?"

I scanned the empty streets. The first haze of dusk was enfolding the trees. "I don't know. I really cocked up, Dehan."

She shrugged. "If you did, we both did. I agreed with your plan. I don't see what else we could have done." She shrugged and shook her head at the same time. "Who could have foreseen he'd run? What the hell did he run for? Where could he be safer? And he had the chance of a deal . . ."

"Doesn't make much sense. What the hell was he looking for?"

The voice came from behind us, at the top of the steps. Father Sullivan stood looking down at us, a black shadow against the arch of the church door.

"Confession," he said. "And absolution."

SEVENTEEN

By the time we got back to St. Mary's, dusk was turning to evening and the CSI team had set up a string of arc lights over the dig. It was an eerie sight, with the guys in their plastic suits appearing and disappearing behind the screens, in the glow of the lamps against the church wall. We ducked under the tape and made our way along the footpath. We could see they had dug four trenches at right angles to each other, and the team was about waist deep in them.

The uniformed cops had removed their jackets and had their shirtsleeves rolled up. They looked tired. Dehan quickened her pace and pointed but I had already seen it. There was a large plastic sheet laid out, and on the sheet there were bones.

Frank saw us approaching and climbed out of the trench. He held up one hand as though to stop me.

"Before you ask me, John, I don't know. At this juncture, I know what you know—you predicted they'd be here, and they are. So that tells you something, but not much. As to the bones, whom they belong to, whether they are male or female, what age, how many . . ." He shook his head. "Don't bother asking me because I don't know, and I won't know until I get them back to the lab." He pointed at the sheet. "You can look, but you can't touch. Now, I have to get back to work."

He didn't wait for an answer. He turned and hurried back to the trench. Dehan and I moved to the plastic sheet. There were two skulls. They were small. There were a few bones that might have been ribs. Nothing more.

"Is one of them Alicia?" I looked sharply at Dehan. She had tears in her eyes. "I used to play dolls with her when we were kids. Is that her, there?" She turned to look at me. Her eyes were large and dark, and amber light of the arc lamps was reflected in her tears.

I had no answer for her. No explanation.

"Let's get out of here, Stone. They've got this."

"Sure."

We walked back toward the gates. Evening was shutting down and night was closing in. I glanced over and saw lights in the rectory. It looked like the kitchen. She put her hand on my shoulder. "Let's have a word with Mrs. Doyle before we leave, she might have heard something."

The door was open and we went in. We found her in the kitchen, sitting at the long pine table staring at a mug of tea. She looked up but didn't say anything. Dehan smiled at her. "You got one of those for a couple of tired cops?"

Mrs. Doyle didn't smile. She looked back at her mug and said, "In the pot, love. Help yourself."

Dehan glanced at me. I shook my head. She poured herself a mug and we sat. I said, "No word?"

She shook her head. Then, in exasperation, "Sure, where would he go? His family's all back home in Ireland, them that's still livin', most of them are dead, God rest their souls. Amn't I all he's got? The feckin' old fool! God forgive me for sayin' it but he is, so he is."

Dehan smiled. "He'd been at Father Sullivan's. You were right about that, but he left just before we arrived. Where do you think he'd go from Father Sullivan's?"

"Isn't that what I'm tellin' you? There is nowhere for him to go. I made him his favorite stew an' all."

"I saw you making it. It looked good. Every cop in New York is on the lookout for him, Mrs. Doyle, even at the airports, shipping ports, railway stations . . . He'll show up sooner or later."

She didn't look very convinced. "I'll have somethin' to say to the silly feckin' eejit when he does."

"You'll let me know the minute he does?"

It was as though I hadn't spoken. She stared into my face with total incomprehension. "Where, in the name of all that's holy, is he going to go? Where is he going to sleep? Who's going to feed the silly gobshite?"

Dehan finished her tea and we stepped back into the night. We crossed the gravel drive to the sidewalk, and I leaned on the roof of the Jag. She came and leaned next to me.

"He's going to come back here, isn't he?"

I nodded. "He had a crisis of conscience, or faith, or whatever religious people have. He's in fear for his life and he needed to confess, to make peace with his creator before he died. Now he's alone in the city. He's scared and he's going to get cold and hungry. He will come home."

She nodded. "He's all we've got to connect the bones to Sadiq Khan, Bishop Bellini, and the others. If he dies, the case dies with him."

"I know."

"We have to stay."

I looked into her face. "You okay? You want to go? I can stay."

She shook her head, and as she did it, I saw the car parked fifty yards away under a plane tree. The young April leaves cast dappled shadows in the limpid light of the streetlamp, but you could see it was white. It was a white Ford Ka. I pointed at it and suddenly knew where he was. Dehan ran for the car; I began to walk back toward the church.

She caught up with me at the steps.

"The car is empty."

The great wooden doors were unlocked and I pushed them open. The huge nave was in darkness, except for four candles that burned at the altar, illuminating the statues of the saints, the elaborate gold leaf, the frescoes, and the giant crucifix. There was absolute silence. Father O'Neil was on his knees in front of his tortured, weeping lord, a bent, broken figure in black. I walked down the central aisle and stood behind him. He was hunched forward, his hands clasped in prayer in his lap.

He had died as he had lived, on his knees, but he had died as he had wanted to die, making peace with his God. It would have been quick, and virtually painless. There was barely a mark on him, save for the small puncture mark at the base of his skull.

Dehan sat on the pew behind him and looked at me.

"We're fucked, Stone." Her eyes traveled down to gaze at him where he knelt, and she almost echoed my thoughts. "He died as he lived, fucking things up for everybody else."

I pulled out my cell and dialed the captain.

"Stone! Did you find him?"

"Yeah. He went to confess with his pal Father Sullivan, then came back to St. Mary's, where he was killed with an ice pick while he was praying."

"He was murdered?"

I closed my eyes and counted to ten before answering. I wanted to tell him, no, it was a freak accident, he fell backward onto an ice pick while kneeling in prayer at the altar. Instead, I said, "Yes, Captain, he was murdered." I didn't add that that was the usual way to acquire an ice pick in your brain.

"And this happened with fifteen cops on the premises?"

"Yeah, they are kind of busy at the moment, digging up skeletons."

"How is that going? Have they found any?"

"When I last checked they had two skulls and several ribs. It is painstaking work."

"I know."

"Nobody is to blame, Captain."

"Okay, Stone. I'll have a team sent over; meanwhile, seal the area."

We took a reel of yellow tape from the CSI truck and sealed the church. Dehan told the cop on duty we had a second crime scene and followed me back to the rectory to give Mrs. Doyle the news.

EIGHTEEN

THEY WORKED THROUGH THE NIGHT, AND ALL through the following day. They recovered a total of fourteen bodies, more than I had expected. Frank had the remains taken to his lab where he and his team carefully, painstakingly, started to reassemble the bones into skeletons. After that, the slow, detailed process of analysis would begin, to establish the age and sex of each one, and if possible, the cause of death. It could take weeks.

All he was able to tell me, after they had started assembling the skeletons, was that it was very unlikely that there were any boys, and that only one of the skulls appeared to be over fifteen years of age.

Alicia.

Dehan went to see her aunt, to give her the news and to ask for Alicia's dental records. She asked me not to accompany her, so I spent the time tracking down Sadiq Khan, then called Bishop Bellini's office. Sadiq Khan was out of the office, and Bishop Bellini was out of the country.

Joe, the CSI team leader who had processed the scene of Father O'Neil's murder, called to tell me what I already knew. It had been a very professional job. There was not a trace of the killer. His spinal cord had been severed at the base, where it met the brain, with a single thrust of a small, sharp blade, probably an ice pick.

Dehan came back about four in the afternoon and dropped into her chair.

"I sent Frank the details so he can contact her insurance company. He said he'd give her priority, as a favor. We should know soon."

I nodded. After a bit, I said, "We seem to have hit a dead end. We uncovered all this from a haircut and a manicure, but I can't see a way of linking what happened to the people who did it."

She leaned back in her chair and rolled her head. I heard her vertebrae crunch.

"Mick is dead, Father O'Neil is dead, that leaves, who? Sadiq Khan . . ."

"Out of the office."

"The bishop . . ."

"Out of the country."

"'H' . . ."

"Untouchable until we have more evidence."

"And Conor Hagan."

I sighed. "Conor Hagan . . ." I reached in the file and pulled out the two emails and the list and placed them on the desk. "He isn't on the list."

"Goddamn it, Stone!" I looked at her. "There is no evidence! How can you investigate a case where there is no evidence? It's twelve years ago!" She mimicked, "'Where were you on the night of the fifteenth of January, twelve years ago?'"

"Hmmm . . . You'd need somebody with a superb memory." I picked up my phone and called Hagan Construction.

"Hagan Construction, how may I . . ."

"This is Detective Stone of the NYPD. I need to talk to Conor Hagan on a very urgent matter, now."

"Thank you, caller, please hold the line while I try to connect you."

I put the phone on speaker, picked up a pencil, and methodically broke it into matchwood. Then a voice like talking concrete emerged from my cell.

"This is Conor. What do you want, Stone."

"I need to talk to you. This is important for both of us."

"I'm at the Shamrock."

"Will you still be there when I get there?"

"Yes."

He hung up. I picked up the folder of photographs.

He was at the same table when we arrived. He was still studying papers and he still had a Guinness, but this time, instead of a beef sandwich he had a whiskey chaser. As we approached, he looked up and nodded at the bartender. We sat.

"I'm guessing you know that Father O'Neil was murdered the night before last?"

He nodded.

"Do you know who did it?"

"I don't murder priests."

"That's not what I asked you. I asked you if you knew who did do it."

"I've no idea."

"We have reason to believe—good reason to believe—that his murder is connected to Sean O'Conor's murder."

"What's that got to do with me?"

"I'm coming to that, Conor. My partner thinks I am crazy, maybe I am, but my gut tells me that whatever you might be, and whatever you might do, you didn't do this."

"Am I supposed to be fucking grateful?"

I nodded. "Yeah. Because Sean's murder turned out to be about a hell of a lot more than squatters."

His eyes narrowed. "Like what?"

The bartender came over with two pints of Guinness and set them in front of us. "It's on the house," he said, and returned to the bar.

I raised my glass to Conor and said, "Slánta." He nodded and turned to Dehan. She had the good sense to do the same.

She sipped and said, "You were putting money into his relief program, and to provide shelter for the people you were evicting from the building on Tiffany Street, and education for the children. There were a few other people who were putting money into that program too. But the program, and the kids, were being exploited and used for something else."

His eyes went hard, his face slowly flushed red, and his breathing grew heavier. This was anger, not fear.

"What are you telling me?"

I showed him the list of names. "This is a list that Sean made. These people are all people involved with the program, but your name is missing."

He pulled the list over and studied it. "Who are these two?"

He pointed to the two decayed names.

I raised my eyebrows. "Who do you think they are?"

"This one is that cunt Mick Harragan. This one I have no idea."

"You know the others?"

"That's the bishop, and Sadiq I've met, but I didn't know he was involved in the program. What fucking interest could he have in helping Catholic kids and educating them in the Catholic faith?"

"None," I said, and pulled out the first photograph, where the kids were all standing together, fully clothed. I slid it across to him. "Do you know who these kids are?"

He studied the picture and after a while, he nodded. "I'm not fucking Mother Teresa, Stone. You know who I am and what I am, and I'll be damned if I pretend to be anything else. I didn't go and fawn over the kids and pretend to be a fucking saint so they could praise me and thank me. I'm a bad man and I'll probably go to hell. So be it. But I didn't want them sleeping on the streets, going into prostitution, getting hooked on drugs. They were only kids. I don't deal in fucking child prostitution or drugs, and I don't hurt children. Okay?" He sighed and looked back at the picture. "Sure, I remember these kids, most of them. They were on Father O'Neil's program."

I slid the folder across. He opened it. He raised his eyes to glare at me and for a moment I thought he was going to attack me, but he looked back at the picture, then methodically worked his way through all twelve of them. I could see his hands were shaking and his chest was rising and falling hard. Dehan decided to add some fuel to the fire.

"Their remains were dug up from Father O'Neil's churchyard yesterday and the night before. Among them were the remains of my cousin, Alicia, who was their teacher."

"Alicia was your cousin?"

Dehan nodded. "And Sean's fiancée."

"What do you want from me?"

I shook my head. "Anything, Conor, anything that will link these bastards with those bones."

His face flushed crimson. "I had no fucking idea that they were doing this. Father O'Neil knew that if I'd had the slightest idea I would have broken every fucking bone in his body, and his pals. Personally! Priest or no fucking priest."

"I believe you, but your anger doesn't help me. I need you to think, remember, was there anything, anything at all at that time that might connect the bishop or Sadiq Khan with these bodies?"

"I already told you. I was not involved personally."

Dehan said, "If we can't prove a connection, Father O'Neil will take the rap and these two, or three, will walk."

He looked at her through hooded eyes. "I know. If I think of anything, I'll give you a bell."

I took a long pull on my Guinness and stood. I gave him a nod. "Thanks for the drink. Don't do anything I wouldn't do."

Dehan stood. Hagan watched me a moment. "I don't know what you wouldn't do."

I held his eye a moment. "Not a lot."

We stepped out into the late-afternoon sunshine and started

walking toward the Jag. Dehan was frowning at her boots as she walked.

"I am not sure what you just did in there, Stone."

I held up a finger and pulled out my cell. I dialed Khan's number. It rang twice and his secretary answered.

"This is Detective Stone of the NYPD. I have a very urgent message for Mr. Sadiq Khan."

"Yes?"

"Tell him that Father O'Neil is dead, that he has been murdered, and that Detective Stone needs to talk to him first thing tomorrow morning. Have you got that?"

"Yes, Detective, I will tell him as soon as he comes in."

"Call him and give him the message."

"Yes, Detective."

Dehan was frowning at me. I smiled and dialed the bishop's number. His secretary answered.

"Bishop Robert Bellini's office."

"This is Detective John Stone of the NYPD. I have an extremely urgent message for the bishop."

"The bishop is out of the country at the moment. He will not be back for a couple of days."

"I know. I need you to get a message of the utmost urgency to him. Tell him Father O'Neil is dead, murdered, and that Detective Stone needs to talk to him as soon as it is physically possible. His life may be in danger, you understand?"

"Yes, Detective, I will communicate your message to him immediately."

Dehan was frowning at me. "What are you doing?"

"If Mohammed can't get to the mountain, then the mountain will have to come to Mohammed."

"That's the wrong way around."

"Everything in this goddamn case is the wrong way around."

NINETEEN

DEHAN FINALLY MADE IT HOME THAT NIGHT. WE WERE both exhausted and needed a few hours thinking about something that wasn't Sean O'Conor, his fiancée, Alicia, and the kids who had died in the church of St. Mary's.

I was thinking of a sirloin steak, French fries, and a glass of wine, watching some mindless crap on the TV. I pushed open my front door and switched on the lights, and my cell rang. I knew who it was. I had been praying he wouldn't call till the morning, but it had been a forlorn hope.

His voice was refined, in a slippery kind of way, with a slight accent.

"Detective Stone?"

"I am guessing you are Sadiq Khan."

"Yes, indeed. I understand you have been desperately trying to reach me." He sounded amused.

"I'm not sure that desperate is quite accurate, Mr. Khan, I am just doing my job, and I have no personal interest in either your safety or your survival. If you haven't either, then we can end this conversation right here and now."

There was a long pause, long enough that I was about to hang up.

"What is this about, Detective? My secretary mentioned a Catholic priest . . ."

I sighed. "Mr. Khan, why don't you can the bullshit and we get down to business? I am tired and, frankly, bored. You are telling me you don't know who Father O'Neil is, so how do you know he was a Catholic priest? If you think I am stupid, Mr. Khan, think again and please stop wasting my time. You put money into his program to rescue children who were being evicted from Conor Hagan's Tiffany Street property. Why does a Muslim businessman invest in a project to teach Catholicism to orphaned kids? There is you, O'Neil, Harragan, and Bellini. I know everything, because before he died, O'Neil told me."

There was another long silence, but this one had a different flavor to it, and I wasn't about to hang up.

"What do you want?"

"I want what Harragan had."

His voice was a sneer. "Well you can only have half of what Harragan had, can't you!"

"What do you mean?"

"You can't screw the pretty Latinas now, can you? They're all dead! You'll have to make do with the money. You cops are all the same."

"That's cute. I'm getting lessons in morality from a pedophile and a murderer."

"I didn't . . ."

I waited. "You didn't what?"

"Never mind. How much do you want?"

"To keep my mouth shut, I want twenty thousand dollars in used bills. Tomorrow at noon, Barretto Point Park, at the amphitheater. I'll be sitting on the top step."

He was sneering again. "Will you have a carnation in your lapel, Detective?"

"No, but I will have my snub-nose .38, and if I even suspect that you have been talking to Bellini, you'll be joining O'Neil in hell a damn sight sooner than you expected. Have I made myself plain, Sadiq?"

"How do I know it's not a trap?"

"You don't. You'll just have to put your faith in human greed. Think you can do that?"

"And what do I get for these twenty thousand dollars? I want more than silence."

I let the smile seep into my voice. "A long and beautiful relationship, outside of Riker's Island."

"I want something, Stone, something concrete. I don't want this hanging over me for the next . . ."

I cut across him. "We'll talk tomorrow. Noon. I'll be with my partner. You come alone or there is no deal." I hung up.

I played back the conversation. It had recorded successfully. I emailed it to myself at work and cc'd Dehan. Then I called her. She sounded sleepy. I could hear *Walker Texas Ranger* in the background.

"No, I will not come and cook you dinner."

"We have him. I recorded the conversation on my phone. I emailed it to you. We have Sadiq Khan in the bag."

She was quiet for a moment. "What are you . . . like . . . magic?"

"Must be."

"You're lucky you're over there, I might embarrass you."

"You having a glass of wine?"

"Mm-hm."

"Good, have one for me. I'll have one for you. Sleep well, Carmen."

"G'night, Sensei."

THE CAPTAIN STARED at my phone on his desk and listened to the conversation. When it had finished, he shook his head in disbelief. Dehan was grinning at her boots. He looked at her and back at me.

"I have to hand it to you, Stone, you seem to have a bottomless bag of tricks. You are sailing damn close to the wind. His defense attorneys are going to be screaming entrapment to high heaven."

I shook my head. "I didn't induce him to commit a crime, Captain, I simply got him to admit that he had."

He nodded. "You'll need backup."

"No, Dehan will be there with me. I don't want to spook him. It has to look like the real deal. We can bring him in. He'll be alone."

He gave me a look. "Don't lose this one, Stone. You have dragged triumph from the jaws of defeat. Don't screw it up!"

"I won't."

"We won't."

We both looked at Dehan. I smiled. "We won't."

"Okay, so you bring him in, you charge him, right? Tell me you are going to charge him."

"We charge him. Let him believe we have a full confession from Father O'Neil, but let him believe also that the evidence is thin against Bellini. If he gives us Bellini, we cut him a deal."

The captain sighed. "The bishop. I don't mind telling you I am going to catch some flak because of this."

Dehan fixed him with her eye. "Sir, with all due respect, anyone who wants to defend that son of a bitch isn't worth listening to. He colluded in the rape and murder of children."

"You are right, of course, Detective. But politics is rarely that simple. Anyway, you know you have my full support, whatever the political consequences."

We thanked him and left.

IT WAS a short drive in the spring sunshine. We took Bruckner over the bridge and then Garrison and Tiffany Street all the way down to Viele Avenue. Even the Hunts Point industrial estate looked pretty, in some ghastly way, in the spring morning light.

We left the car in the lot outside the park, in the shade of the maples, and strolled down to the water's edge. We had fifteen minutes to spare, so we sat on the rocks and stared out at the East River. I had that feeling I often had with Dehan, that she had somehow managed to get inside my mind, or she was already a part of it.

"Will he show?"

I gave a small shrug. "You heard him. He was real motivated last night."

She picked up a small stone and threw it out into the water. It hit the river with a hollow *plock*.

"If we lose him that will only leave the bishop."

"And 'H.'"

"You know who 'H' is, don't you?"

I gave a few small nods. "Probably. But so do you."

"I think so."

"What do we do if Khan doesn't show, Stone?"

I studied her face. She looked lost. She looked as though she was reaching out to me for a way forward.

"That depends on why he doesn't show." I looked at my watch. It was five to. "Let's go."

We climbed the steps of the amphitheater to the top. I sat, and Dehan stood staring back along the path toward the entrance to the park. Noon came and slipped into afternoon by five minutes, then ten, then fifteen. At twenty past, I stood and said, "Come on, we have work to do."

She was giving me a weird, searching look. "What work?"

It was a twenty-five-minute drive, though it took a little longer because of the lunchtime traffic. Most people think of the Bronx as a place of ghettos, prostitution, and crime. They are right; much of the Bronx is like that, but not all of it. Riverdale is one part of the Bronx that is definitely not a ghetto. And that was where Sadiq Khan had his house, on West 232nd Street, opposite Seton Park. It was a green, leafy suburb of large, luxurious houses and small mansions. It wasn't Oyster Bay, but it wasn't Hunts Point either.

Sadiq's house was a three-story, oddly angular building painted an unpleasant shade of sage green. It was set back from the road beyond a sweeping lawn. I could see a C-Class Mercedes and a Citroen Clio in the drive. Something told me the Clio was his wife's.

I pulled in and parked in front of them. I killed the engine and we climbed out. Dehan peered through the windows at the front, and I rang the bell. There was total silence apart from the sporadic singing of the birds.

If they had kids, they'd be at school. Maybe his wife was shopping, but if she was, why didn't she take her car? And why was his car still in the drive? And if both cars were in the drive, why was nobody answering the door?

Dehan wandered back to me with her hands in her back pockets. "There's nobody at home, Stone."

I shook my head and pointed at the Merc and the Citroen. "Nobody is answering. That's different. Besides, I think I hear somebody shouting, or calling out, don't you?"

She raised an eyebrow at me. "Yeah, I thought I heard a woman shouting 'help.'"

"Good, me too."

I went around to the kitchen door at the back, smashed the glass with my elbow, and reached in to unlock the door. It grated on the shattered glass as I pushed it open. Dehan had her piece in her hand as she followed me in. The glass crunched under her boots. It sounded really loud in the stillness.

The living room was empty. There were no pictures on the walls, no ornaments, no bookcases. There was a gray carpet, a gray sofa, a vast glass-and-brass coffee table, and a TV the size of a cinema screen. A curving staircase, also carpeted in gray, led to the upper floor. We climbed it, listening for some sound, some sign of life. There wasn't any.

We came to a landing. The door to the bathroom stood open, and I saw a mug with four toothbrushes in it. I touched Dehan's shoulder and pointed at it. She nodded. She looked a little sick. The first door we opened was obviously one of the kid's rooms. It was painted pastel blue and there was a princess bed with a lace net hung over it. Mrs. Khan and her two daughters were sitting on the floor. The girls were wearing school uniforms. Their ankles and their wrists, like their mother's, were bound with duct tape, and they had duct tape over their mouths. Their eyes were huge and they looked terrified.

Dehan put her piece away and I showed them my badge. Then I knelt and cut the tape from their wrists and ankles. As Mrs. Khan pulled the tape from her own mouth, she started crying and shouting at me in a language I didn't understand.

I held her shoulders and said, "Mrs. Khan, listen to me. Listen. Detective Dehan is going to take you downstairs. Do you understand? And she is going to call an ambulance. Go with her. Take the children and go downstairs."

She was incoherent, and the kids, taking their cue from their mother, also began to cry. Dehan gathered them up and led them down to the living room. I went to the master bedroom.

He was there, if you could call it him. The bed was saturated with blood. He was naked and badly bruised all over. His body was a pasty gray color because he had pretty much been exsanguinated, but you could see large, yellowish patches where the bruises would have been. His face was grotesquely disfigured and he had several teeth missing. He was also bound hand and foot with tape, as the rest of his family had been.

The blood had come from a single wound. He had been castrated. His entire penis and testicles had been removed and lay next to him on the bed.

I took my phone and dialed the captain.

"Stone. What news?"

"Khan has been murdered and castrated at his house in Riverdale. You'd better talk to the local precinct to sort out jurisdiction. Then we'll need a CSI team and a meat wagon."

"Stone . . . ?"

"Yeah."

"What the hell is going on?"

"Looks like we are running out of people to prosecute."

"Can you even get to the bishop now?" He sounded mad.

I nodded, even though he couldn't see me. "Sure."

TWENTY

WITH THAT ALMOST MATERNAL CARE THAT SEEMED, ON the surface, so at odds with her brash manner and her aggressive attitude, Dehan had sat the Khans on the sofa, wrapped them in blankets, and made them hot, sweet tea. When I got down, the three were shivering with shock and clinging to each other, crying.

I gave Dehan a nod and we stepped into the kitchen.

"They're on their way. He's in the master bedroom. They did a job on him. He was castrated . . ."

For a moment, she almost looked mad. She stared into my face, but her eyes made little shifts, like she was trying to read my features. I gave her a blank page. After a moment, she said, "Completely different to Father O'Neil's murder."

"Yes."

"This was vengeance."

"Looks like it."

"Or punishment . . ."

I nodded. "Or punishment."

She sighed. "So where does this leave us? Bishop Robert Bellini and 'H' get away?"

"I don't see why."

Her face flushed and her open hand shot out, gesturing

toward the stairs. "He was our last chance, Stone! He could have given us the whole ring! He could have told us the whole story!" I gave her a moment. She blurted, "You shouldn't have opened up to Hagan like that! I'm sorry! I have never criticized you before, Stone, but that was a mistake, and it may have lost us the case!"

I nodded. "I can see how you'd think that."

Far off, the wail of a siren stained the air with tragedy. It was incongruous against the green lawn and the spring blue of the sky.

Minutes later, they crammed into the driveway, with their lights flashing, and began to disgorge men and women in uniform who went, with mechanical precision, about the task of processing a scene where four lives had been destroyed. The yellow tape went up, the ME arrived with her black bag, the CSI team climbed into their plastic suits and tramped, like something out of a sci-fi B movie, around the wreckage of Mrs. Khan's home. And meanwhile, Mrs. Khan and her two little girls sobbed and struggled to assimilate the impossible.

I showed Lisa, the ME, up to the room. It was bad enough to make her stop in the doorway and wince. Dehan came in after her. She shook her head and turned to stare at me, like it was my fault.

Lisa said, "I can tell you straightaway the cause of death was exsanguination. Anything else will have to wait till I get back to the lab."

I met Greg, the CSI team leader, on the stairs on his way up. We stopped and his team filed past us, headed for the two bedrooms.

"I'm guessing there was more than one of them, Greg. Nobody seems to have put up a fight, and they were able to bind him, the wife, and the kids without resistance before separating them into two rooms. We didn't find any sign of forced entry, so I'm guessing maybe they waited till the family was leaving for school and work. The doors are open, they're all out in the drive, and they came up, blocked the exit, and forced them back into the house, maybe at gunpoint. Mrs. Khan will confirm that later, right now she is in no state."

He listened carefully, then gave a nod. "Okay, see what we can find."

He went on up after his team. I knew they wouldn't find anything.

When we got back down, Mrs. Khan had settled a little and was drinking her tea. Dehan went and sat next to her.

"Can you tell me what happened, Mrs. Khan? I know it's hard, but the sooner you can tell us, the sooner we can catch whoever did this."

It was as I had thought.

"We were going to school." She gestured at her daughters. "I always drive them. Is not far. Sadiq . . ." Her eyes flooded and her face flushed. Her breath shook. Dehan took her hand. ". . . He said he had an important appointment at midday. We were all standing together, in the drive, and then a big SUV came into the drive. It blocked our way, there was no way out. And two men got out. They were very big. They wore black sweatshirts, black jeans, all black, and black balaclavas over their faces. They were holding guns. They forced us inside. Upstairs."

"Did they say anything?"

"Nothing, not a word. One of them bound us and locked us in the bedroom. Then he went next door . . ." Her face collapsed and she started to sob. "We heard horrible noises, Sadiq screaming . . ."

We called her doctor and had him come out to sedate her. Then we called her sister to come and take care of her. After that, we stepped out to the Jag and I negotiated my way past the patrol cars and the meat wagon onto the road. I headed east toward the Deegan Expressway.

We drove in silence, but it wasn't the silence I was used to. It was an uncomfortable silence. Eventually, I asked her, "Have you lost confidence in me, Dehan?"

She looked away from me, out the side window.

"I don't know." She turned to face me for a second, and then looked away again. "I don't understand. I get why you left Father O'Neil to sweat. It made sense to me, and there was no way we could have known he was going to run to Father Sullivan."

"But...?"

"But I don't get . . ." Now she shifted in her seat to face me, gesturing back at the house with her hand. "You knew that Conor Hagan would react like this! I didn't! It didn't cross my mind. But you! Shit, Stone! You are the sensei! You knew! And now I am asking myself, why the hell did we go there and have that conversation with Hagan? Why the hell did you show him those photographs?"

I glanced at her to see if she had finished. She was waiting.

"I had to be sure."

"Sure of what?"

"That he wasn't part of it."

She made little shakes with her head in a "what the hell are you talking about?" gesture.

I sighed. "It could be one of two ways, Dehan. Either Hagan was a part of it or he wasn't. If he was, we had a very different kind of setup on our hands. You saw him, you spoke to him, and this guy is a damn good administrator. He is efficient and he rules with an iron fist. He has never been arrested. He has never been the subject of an investigation, even though every cop in New York knows he is the head of the Hagan Clan."

She was frowning. That was a good sign. It meant she was thinking. "What's your point?"

"My point is that if Hagan was involved, we were looking at a very well-organized criminal operation involving child prostitution, one that was probably still operational."

"Okay . . ."

"But if he wasn't involved, we were looking at Father O'Neil, an incompetent fool, we were looking at Mick Harragan, who relied on violence, terror, and low cunning, but didn't have a fraction of Hagan's intelligence—and in any case has been dead for the last ten years—we were looking at a businessman and a bishop, both of whom were dabbling, and 'H,' all three of whom needed to remain as uninvolved as possible. A very different proposition, Dehan, a small group of sick pedophiles, with no competent organizer at the head."

"So you confronted Conor to see how he would react."

I turned off West 230th onto the Deegan Expressway and began to accelerate.

"I was pretty sure by then that Hagan was not involved, but I needed to be sure."

"Did he kill Father O'Neil?"

I shook my head. "I don't think so. Why would he?"

"But you must have been aware of the risk that Hagan would come after Sadiq!"

I frowned at her. "Dehan, I need you to think this through. This gang of pedophiles, who were prepared to murder fourteen young girls to conceal their crime, cheated one of the most dangerous men in New York, one of the most dangerous gangs in the country. He donated money, probably tens of thousands of dollars, to the care and education of these girls, and they used that money to enslave, rape, and murder them. And you think that it was my actions that put Sadiq at risk." She turned away from me and stared straight ahead at the expressway without answering. After a bit, I glanced at her. "I have never lied to you, Dehan, and I never will. So I have to say to you that, in the first place, I don't think it was my actions that put him and his family at risk, I think it was his actions. And in the second place, if it was, I don't honestly give a good goddamn. He had it coming."

She didn't talk again until we were approaching the junction with the Cross Bronx Expressway.

"Just tell me this, Stone, did you deliberately have him executed?"

She watched my face as I answered. "No, but I knew Hagan might. I weighed it up, Dehan. In the end, I followed the investigation in the way I had to, and Sadiq had to face the consequences of his own actions."

The second call came as we were approaching the 43rd. I put it on speaker and laid it on the dash.

"Stone."

"Detective Stone, I believe you have been trying to contact me." The voice was cultured, and supremely arrogant. "This is Bishop Robert Bellini."

I waited a beat, and then asked him, "Can you speak freely, Bishop?"

"Yes, I am alone."

"Good, are you back in the States?"

"Why don't you tell me what it is you want, Detective?"

"You heard that Father O'Neil was murdered."

"So I am told."

"Were you also told that Sadiq Khan has been murdered too?" He didn't answer. I gave him a minute and went on. "Were you also told that the bodies of the girls have been dug up from the churchyard? I tell you, Bellini, you step out of the country for a couple of days and all hell breaks loose."

I waited, but he still didn't speak.

"You don't want to talk to me, Bellini, that's fine."

I reached out to hang up and his voice, rich with contempt, said, "What do you want, Stone?"

"People keep asking me that these days. What do I want? I want to see you in person and talk to you."

"What for?"

"Well, you see, I figure we can do this one of two ways. I can be Detective John Stone, the ruthless, unrelenting investigator who always gets his man, or I can be a friend to you and to the Church."

"What makes you think I need a friend?"

I sighed loudly. "I haven't got time to fuck around playing your stupid games, Bishop. Call me when you're ready to talk sense."

I reached over and hung up. I pulled into the parking lot and killed the engine. Dehan was staring at me with no expression. I counted to nine and the phone rang.

"Stone."

"I need a little more than your words."

"You, Mick Harragan, Sadiq Khan, and . . ." I paused. "Let's just call him 'H' while we're on the phone. O'Neil made a full confession. I am sitting on that confession for now. But on the strength of it, I dug up the churchyard. We've found the bodies of fourteen young girls; we also found photographs that Sean O'Conor was holding, of the twelve girls who made up the first class that Alicia was going to teach. Father O'Neil identified the girls . . . Shall I carry on, or is that enough for now?"

"It's enough."

"Listen to me, you piece of shit. Mick Harragan was your friend. Now I am your friend, you understand me? The big difference is that Mick was stupid and I am not. Now, if you play your cards right, we can make this profitable, and a lot of fun for everybody involved. Play them wrong, Bellini, and I will hit you so hard your fucking head will be spinning for a week."

"Very well, you are my friend. Now what?"

"We meet."

"Where and when?"

"In your office. I don't want to be seen with you in public. I have legitimate reason to come and see you to discuss Father O'Neil. When are you back?"

He sighed. "I am at the airport now."

I felt a sudden wave of disgust. "I had a feeling you might be. I'll see you this afternoon, at four. And Bellini?"

"What?"

"I want you to think long and hard about this. Have you any idea what they do to men like you in prison?"

He was quiet for a moment. Then, he said, "I am not going to prison, Stone."

He hung up. I played it back, and we listened to what he'd

said with care. When it was finished, Dehan shook her head. "It's not enough. He doesn't want to incriminate himself."

"I agree. We'll see what we get this afternoon. Right now, there is one thing we have to come out with from his office."

"What?"

I lifted up my hand and wiggled my fingers. "Prints."

She nodded once. "Yes . . ."

"I am going to scare the bejaysus out of him. I am going to make crazy demands and blackmail him. While he's focusing on that, I'm going to get his prints."

She nodded and said, "It's a good plan." Then she climbed out of the car, slammed the door, and walked inside.

TWENTY-ONE

WHEN I GOT INSIDE, DEHAN WAS SITTING AT HER DESK. She was on the phone and writing something on a piece of paper. I dropped into my chair.

She said, "And he is willing to talk to us . . ." She nodded a couple of times, then said, "Thank you, Mr. Foster. That's very helpful."

She hung up. She drew breath to tell me what it was about but I interrupted her.

"Have we got a problem?"

"Yes."

"Is it going to jeopardize the investigation?"

She stared at me hard and seemed about to say something, then stopped herself. Finally, she said, "I don't know."

I tried to keep the anger from my voice but didn't do a great job.

"How long is it going to take you to find out?"

She sighed. "That was David Foster."

"I know who it was."

"He managed to track down . . ."

"Arnav Singh and he is willing to talk to us, I got that."

I saw tears spring to her eyes, and she gestured at the paper in front of her. "I have his number . . ."

I watched her face a moment. I felt a sudden rush of irritation, which was probably more fear than anger. "You going to call him, or shall I?"

She picked up the paper and tossed it over to me. Then she stood up and walked out. She might have gone to the toilet or she might have gone to the captain. It was impossible to tell. I dialed the number. It rang twice and a very pleasant, cultured voice that could almost have been English said, "This is Arnav Singh."

"Mr. Singh, this is Detective John Stone of the NYPD."

"Ah, David said you might call. Look here, I'd rather not have this conversation over the telephone." He laughed in a self-deprecating way and added, "And please don't use any buzzwords. I am a little paranoid, let's meet."

"Where are you?"

"I'm in Washington. Can you come here?"

"Yeah. Tomorrow?"

"Good. Do you know the National Gallery Gardens on Madison Drive Northwest?"

"Sure."

"There's a café, the Pavilion. I'll meet you there. One p.m."

He hung up.

I spent twenty minutes tapping a pencil on my desk and spinning it in my fingers. Dehan came back with two beef sandwiches and two cups of coffee. She put one of each in front of me and started to eat. I looked at mine a second and felt sick.

"Are you coming to see the bishop?"

"Of course."

"I thought maybe you'd gone to see the captain."

She shook her head.

"I phoned Arnav Singh."

"What did he say?"

"He's in DC. I arranged to go and see him tomorrow at one p.m. I figure on the I-95 it should be four hours, four and a half at most." She nodded and ate in silence. "So I thought I'd leave about seven, beat the traffic, and have a look around before he arrives. It's not likely to be a trap in such a public place, but still, with two witnesses dead, I'd like to see him arrive, and see who arrives before him and with him."

"Makes sense."

"You going to be there?"

"Yes, of course. Stop asking that."

I sighed and picked up my sandwich. I didn't feel like eating but I forced myself.

BISHOP ROBERT BELLINI'S offices were on the top floor of a large, Gothic building on Beach Avenue, beside the Church of the Sacred Heart of Jesus. We were led up six flights of stairs by a lackey in a black hassock who tapped reverently on the huge, studded oak door and opened it to announce us. As he stepped in, he said, "Your Excellency, Detectives Stone and Dehan to see you."

I heard him mutter something, and the lackey stepped aside to let us in.

Bellini was handsome the way Italian men are handsome. He was short and had tight black hair that was graying at the temples. He was dressed in a black suit that was probably from Armani's Bishops line, a black shirt from their Mafia line, and a dog collar from their special Sub-Dom line. He was standing by a window that was considerably taller than he was, and watched us come in. He studied Dehan with prurient eyes.

"I thought you would come alone."

"Did you deal with Mick, or with Mick and Kirk?"

He didn't answer but strutted behind his vast mahogany desk and settled into an equally vast black leather chair.

"Michael Harragan was a well-connected man. I have made some inquiries about you, Detective Stone. You are not a well-connected man."

"Yeah? Who did you ask, the Pope?"

"People who take an especial interest in the affairs of the Bronx. There is a long-standing Italian community in the Bronx, Detective Stone. Somebody has to look out for their interests, keep an eye on them and protect them."

"The way the girls at Father O'Neil's orphan program were protected?"

"That was very lamentable."

"Lamentable?" It was Dehan.

He smiled at her without warmth while he undressed her with his eyes. "Sadly," he said, "it is human nature to give in to the appetites of the flesh. It is not for us to judge, however, but to offer up prayers and beg for forgiveness for our own sins."

Before Dehan could answer, I said, "Are you done? Because I have had a bellyful of bullshit. Are we going to do business or what?"

He sighed deeply and pulled one of those expressive Italian faces where the eyebrows go all the way up and the mouth goes all the way down.

"Business, Detective, what are you selling?"

"Our silence and cooperation. You interested or not?"

He shrugged like he couldn't give a damn.

"I hear a lot of talk, but I have not seen anything. Where is this confession? You have even a copy of it? What are you going to take to the DA? What are you going to adduce in court? Your word? The word of two corrupt police officers against the word of the Roman Catholic Bishop of the Diocese of St. Mary's?"

I sat forward. "Let me ask you something, Bellini, do I look stupid? You think I am stupid enough to bring O'Neil's confession to your little Mafia HQ? You think I don't know you're in bed with Vincenzo? The confession stays where it is until I see the cash. A copy? You want a fucking copy? What am I, your fucking office boy? I have every word of his confession in my head. You want me to run through it for you? You want to discuss the details of what you and those fucking animals did to those little girls? Or would you rather see it reported in the *New York Times* tomorrow morning?"

He was cool. He wasn't shaken. He watched me with dead eyes and said nothing. He was smarter than Sadiq by a long chalk, but he hadn't made up his mind that I was bluffing either. In the end, he said, "I need more than your word."

"It's all you're getting till I see your money."

"How do I know I can trust you?"

"Trust me? What's the matter with you? You can't trust me. That's why I'm here, because I'm bent. Make your arrangements, cover your back, do what you have to do, but I want my money, and I want involvement, you understand me?"

"What do you mean, you want involvement?"

I put a big smile on the side of my face. "I want you dirty, Bellini. I am not dealing with intermediaries. I am putting my career, and my life on the line here, and so is my partner. You commit too. If one of us goes down, we all three go down. And any business you and Vincenzo conduct in the Bronx, I'm a part of it. I told you, I want what Mick had."

He didn't look awfully impressed. "I need to think about it."

"Seriously, you need to think about it?" I stood and pointed at him. "You're a fucking asshole. You're not useless to me, Bellini. You will be useful as an example to those who come after you, and to Vincenzo. Make sure you get the *New York Times* tomorrow, and expect a visit from the DA."

Dehan stood. Bellini held up a hand.

"Wait. How much do you want?"

"For what?"

He frowned. There was suspicion in his eyes. I laughed. "I want a one-off payment, then there is the retainer, and then there are percentages on the jobs. What are you talking about?"

He nodded once, and then hesitated. "The one-off payment for the confession."

I sat back in my chair. I was aware the meeting was coming to an end and I still didn't have his prints.

"Fifty grand in used bills."

He closed his eyes and sighed. "Where and when?"

I thought about it a moment. "Ferry Point Park, corner of Emerson Avenue and Shurz Avenue, by the river. You know it?"

He gave a weary nod. "I know of it. When?"

I was suddenly tired. I looked at Dehan. She was staring at the bishop, like she was entranced by some movie. I forced myself to focus. The next day we were going to be eight or nine hours driving, plus however long we spent in DC. We wouldn't be back before four or five at the earliest, and we might need time to consider whatever Singh gave us.

"Day after tomorrow. Ten a.m."

"All right, Stone. But be aware, I will have you both executed at the earliest chance I have."

"Good to know." I turned to Dehan. "Anything you want to add?"

She caught the irony in my tone, looked at me a moment, and shook her head. She stood and we left.

TWENTY-TWO

THE STREETLAMPS WERE COMING ON WHEN WE GOT downstairs, but the sky was still light. I walked to the Jag and got in. She got in beside me. She didn't slam the door. She closed it softly. I fired up the engine and drove straight up Beach Avenue for a block and parked just before the junction with Westchester. When I stopped and killed the engine, she looked at me with a query on her face. I ignored her and got out. She got out after me and we crossed the road to the South of France. A bar that is hideous to look at on the outside, but good enough to drink in on the inside.

I ordered two beers and took them to a table. I put one in front of her. She said, "You didn't get the prints."

I ignored her and said, "This place closes at two a.m. But we are not leaving until we have resolved this. So talk."

She heaved a sigh and slid back in her chair.

She took a long pull and then set about making interlocking rings on the tabletop with the base of her glass.

"It's hard for me to talk about this kind of stuff."

I looked at my watch. "We have eight hours. If necessary, we can continue at my place."

"Stone, you are the first and only person I have ever trusted, apart from my parents. I was a weird kid from a weird family growing up in a tough neighborhood where weird kids were not welcome. I learned early, real early, not to trust people. Not to trust anybody but my mom and my dad. I made an exception with you."

She paused and made a few more interlocking rings, like she was trying to link her thoughts. When she spoke again, she was staring at the table.

"Stone, my mom and dad were murdered, destroyed body and soul, by a bent cop. Not just a bent cop, a cop who was sadistic and cruel and violent. When I met you, when we were partnered, you were everything that Mick Harragan was not. In your own, dinosaur way you were honorable, decent, good . . ."

"Stop, you're going to make me blush."

She didn't laugh. "It's not a joke, Stone, it meant a lot to me. I felt I could trust you. I never got that close to anybody before." She looked back at the table for a moment, like she had her thoughts laid out there. "You were tough, you had attitude, you could be as mean as the next guy when you had to be, but the bottom line, I always knew you were going to do the right thing. You were honorable."

I took a pull of my beer. "All of this is in the past tense."

She gave her head a shake, but it wasn't a denial. It was a shake of reluctance. "I don't recognize you, this you I have seen in the last couple of days, this you that fed Conor Hagan information that would get Sadiq killed, that exposed his daughters to a trauma from which they will never recover. And now you have set Bellini up for the same fate. You're not taking him into protective custody, you're not arresting him. But you know Hagan is going to come after him. Suddenly, I don't know you."

I smiled and rubbed my face with my hands. It was ironic, and I let that show on my face. "Couple of days ago, you made me promise that I would not dump you, or ask the captain for a change of partner. I did promise, and I will stick by that promise, because, though I am fallible, like any human being, what you said about me is basically true. I try to be honorable, and I try to do the right thing where I can. Now, ironically, it is you who is going to dump me."

"I didn't say that."

"You don't need to. It's written all over you. I may as well have been alone back there in Bellini's office. I didn't get his prints, but neither did you."

"I'm sorry."

"Dehan, if you want me to, I can explain what I did and why I did it, but I am not going to justify it, apologize, or beg you to stay. I want you to stay. You're the best partner I ever had and the best friend. But you have to make your own choices according to your own conscience." I paused and took a deep breath. "I just hope if you do decide to transfer, you know why you're doing it."

She looked hard at me. "What do you mean?"

"Ever since you saw those two girls, when you look at me, you don't see me, you see Mick Harragan. You partner with somebody else, you'll be trying to walk away from Harragan, but you'll be breaking up a damn good partnership, and maybe a friendship with it."

"That's blackmail, Stone."

"No, it's not. It's reality. And that's the difference."

"The difference with what?"

"What Mick did was abuse and brutalize weak, vulnerable people so that he could exploit them for money and sex. And because he was cunning and had no inhibitions, he escaped the law. Remember, Dehan, the justice he received in the end was unlawful. It was Maria who killed him.

"What I do, Carmen, is to try to see things as they really are—not how I want them to be or how the law says they should be, but as they really are. And I saw thirteen girls—more, as it turned out—who had been raped and murdered by this gang of sadistic monsters who felt entitled, because of their power and their privilege, to take these girls' lives. And I saw that they were going to get away with it because all our evidence was either decayed or dead."

Her eyes were locked on my face, but her expression was one of fear, anticipating that I was going to destroy the trust she had put in me, in my care.

"But I did not hand Sadiq—or Bellini—over to Hagan for him to execute them. God knows I would have been justified in doing so. But I didn't. I had two options: shelve the case, file it as unsolved, and betray the memory of those children, your cousin, and Sean O'Conor; or investigate. And investigating meant two things: finding out if I was up against Hagan or not, and exposing Sadiq and Bellini to the risk of being executed by Hagan." I shrugged. "Maybe I am not as honorable as you would like me to be, maybe you are misguided in your idea of what honor is, maybe both are true. But if Sadiq had not raped and murdered those children, or at least colluded in their murder and rape, Conor Hagan would not have gone after him." I picked up my glass. "And besides, I don't see it as any part of my job to protect creatures like Sadiq and Bellini from the consequences of their own actions."

She was quiet for a long time, thinking.

"What about the girls? What about what they witnessed?"

I spread my hands. I felt genuinely helpless. "Dehan, I wasn't able to protect you from Mick Harragan either. How many kids have we failed to protect this year? If we start limiting our investigations because of the collateral damage we might do to a criminal's family, we will end up completely paralyzed. Think what Sadiq would have gone through in prison. How do we protect his daughters from that?"

"It sucks."

I nodded. "Yuh, that is reality, and don't we know it!"

She smiled in a way you could call rueful.

"But Sadiq is not your dad, Mrs. Khan is not your mom, you are not those little girls, and I am definitely not Mick Harragan. For a start, I haven't got four million bucks in an account in Belize."

She looked at me and gave another rueful smile. She sat

forward and put her hand over mine. "Sorry, partner. You're a good man and I shouldn't have doubted you. It was all a bit close to home."

I put my hand over hers. "Hey, don't worry about it. I got your back. What do you say, spaghetti Bolognese, bottle of wine, and an early start?"

She smiled. For a moment she looked really happy. She blinked a couple of times and I realized she was blinking away tears. She nodded, then got up and went quickly to the toilet. I watched her go and thought about all the male partners I had had over the years. I tried to remember any of them ever doing something like that. I was pretty sure none of them ever had.

TWENTY-THREE

WE ARRIVED AT NOON, PARKED ON INDIANA AVENUE, and walked a block back to the park. We had a look around. There were few people, and nobody seemed to have any interest in us. At twelve forty, we found a place for Dehan to sit on the edge of the fountain, where she could cover the entrance to the park and the entrance to the Pavilion Café. Then I went inside and chose a table close by the glass wall where she could see me and I could see her.

She sat cross-legged, tied her hair into a knot at the back of her head, and started looking at her phone. When I was a kid and used to go to the movies, she would have been reading a book or a newspaper, but Orwell's nightmare of a screen for every human being had become a reality in a way he could never have imagined; that people would actually pay for their screens, and carry them around with them voluntarily.

Every few seconds, she looked up and scanned the area. At one o'clock precisely, she looked directly at me and then back at her phone. A few seconds later, a man in a suit appeared. He looked Indian, with olive skin and very black hair. He was in his late thirties or early forties.

He stepped into the café, saw me, and came over. He sat and smiled.

"Don't shake my hand. There is nothing unusual about our meeting here. I meet a lot of friends and acquaintances here."

I leaned back in my chair. "That's fine. Who do you think is watching you?"

He hailed a waitress and shrugged. "Maybe nobody, but in this city, in this job, you learn to be careful. Cappuccino please, Astrid."

This last was directed at the waitress who had rolled over and was smiling at us. I smiled back. "And two double espressos."

He grinned as the waitress rolled away. "Your friend on the fountain." She had got off the wall and was pushing through the door. "She's good. I almost missed her."

She slipped into a chair.

"He came alone."

He nodded. "I did. I came alone. Because I am the only person in the world who knows what I am about to share with you." He smiled apologetically. "It sounds melodramatic, but it is the truth." He laid both hands on the table and seemed to study them for a moment. "Sean and I didn't actually know each other very long. We came from very different backgrounds and had very little in common, but we were both very idealistic." He glanced at each of us in turn. "You understand, we both really wanted to make a difference."

The coffees arrived, and we were instructed by the waitress to enjoy them. Dehan gave a lopsided smile and said, "We've learned enough about Sean in the last few days to believe that much."

"For me, it was always a question of making subtle changes from the inside. Get into the corridors of power and influence change from there." He gave a laugh. "You know? The cynics are as mistaken as the idealists. Politicians are just like the rest of us, neither good nor bad, but somewhere in between. Most people would rather do good, if they can. Most people's sin is not evil, but indifference."

Personally, I prefer to get my philosophy from Hume and Locke than from a guy who spends too much time reading Facebook thought-bites. So I smiled and said, "You were telling us about Sean."

"Yuh, sorry. I get carried away sometimes. Anyway, that was my approach, but Sean." He got a faraway look in his eyes, smiled, and shook his head. "He was the fearless warrior. I don't know if it was that Celtic fire in his blood or what it was, but he had to be reckless and bold, and meet his enemy in open battle. Nothing else would do for him. He was truly fearless."

For a moment, the incongruity of it struck me. This fearless warrior, who was devout almost to the point of fanaticism, who must meet his enemy in open battle, had died on his knees. It somehow didn't seem to fit. I filed it away for further consideration.

"David Foster told us he didn't talk much about his cases."

"That is true. We used to have regular meetings at the Drop-In Center and discuss points of law and give each other a hand. Sean was a very good lawyer, and also a tiny bit arrogant. He would discuss our cases with us, but very rarely confide in us about his. But later, as he and I became closer friends, he did begin to confide in me a bit."

Dehan sipped her coffee. I could tell she was becoming impatient. She said, "About which cases in particular?"

He nodded at her, like she had asked just the right question. "That's it, exactly, it was about two particular cases. The first was the eviction of squatters on Tiffany Street. He was awfully indignant about that. He had several meetings with the Hagan Construction lawyers and he seemed to be pleased with the progress they were making." He paused, frowning. "You know about his fiancée?"

Dehan nodded. "Alicia."

He beamed. "Lovely girl. Lovely! So beautiful, so sweet, so kind, he met her at the Church of St. Mary's, where he was always doing voluntary work, as was she. And straightaway, they hit it off and fell in love. It was a fairy-tale love affair, worthy of a movie, I am telling you. So he made an arrangement with Father O'Neil, with Alicia, and with Conor Hagan, that the Church of St. Mary's would take care of the evicted squatters and provide education for the orphaned children, with Alicia as their loving teacher. Conor Hagan would provide a sum of money. It was considerable, one hundred grand I think was the agreed amount . . ."

"One hundred grand?"

"Oh yes! It was a big sum of money!"

Dehan whistled through her teeth. "No wonder he's mad."

"And a small group of benefactors would match his contribution so that Father O'Neil could provide help for the dispossessed. Of course, their contribution was just on paper. No payment was ever made. They just stole Hagan's money."

I scratched my chin. "So, as far as Sean was concerned, his case against Conor Hagan had been resolved."

"Yes, indeed. That is exactly right. It was always really more a matter of brinkmanship and negotiation than a likely court case."

I turned to Dehan. "Of course, David Foster wouldn't have known that, because Sean didn't discuss his cases with him."

Arnav nodded. "That is correct. Because even as the resolution was found, Sean became extremely worried by things that began to emerge."

Dehan said, "The prostitution ring."

Arnav shook his head. "Oh no, it was not prostitution. It was much worse than prostitution."

Dehan frowned. "Worse?"

He nodded. "They were slaves. They were sex slaves. For the personal use of the cabal, but above all, for clients or political allies that needed to be appeased or coaxed."

I felt sick. "How did he find out about this?"

"It was Alicia. There was a child, her name was Sole. It is ironic; it is the diminutive of 'soledad,' which in Spanish means 'loneliness,' and I have often thought how alone those girls must have felt in those few months that they were there.

"It was Sole, who was only eleven years old, who began to confide in Alicia about the parties that they were taken to at night sometimes."

Dehan spoke tonelessly. "Parties . . ."

"Sometimes Father O'Neil would take them. He would tell them to pray for God's forgiveness!" He looked away, shaking his head. Gathered himself and went on. "He would tell them to pray for God's forgiveness because they were going to be made to sin, but if they repented and prayed for forgiveness, God would still allow them into Heaven."

I asked, "Did he ever participate in these parties?"

"Apparently not, he was just the chauffeur. Other times, some men would come and take them and then bring them back.

"At first Alicia thought that Sole was making it up. The child had had a very traumatic infancy; it would not be uncommon for her to indulge in fantasies sometimes. But then she began to display bruises. When Alicia approached Father O'Neil, he dispelled her concerns, saying that sometimes the girls had squabbles at night, but eventually she began to talk to the other girls. Some of them, the older ones, were too scared to admit that it was true, but some of the younger ones did. And once the young ones did, they all did."

"So what did she do? She didn't go to the cops."

He gave a harsh laugh and looked at me like I was crazy. "No way, Jose! There was a cop in the cabal. One Michael Harragan, a man with a special passion for Latina girls. A very violent and dangerous man at that. He was always at the church, demanding one girl or another, and Alicia was very careful to stay away from him, apparently, because he would have gone for her good and proper, I don't mind telling you!"

Dehan nodded. "So she told Sean?"

"Exactly, and he and I discussed it. We decided that the only thing to do was to get depositions from all the children. So, using various pretexts, such as Sean wanting to check on the progress of the children, he and Alicia worked together, gathering statements from each of the girls, and it was as they did this that they began to realize the extent of what was being done, and the grave danger that all of them—all of us—were in. For not only was the bishop of St. Mary's an active member, but he was intimately connected with the major Mafia crime family of New Jersey, the Vincenzo family. They gathered a lot of evidence, photographs that were taken of the girls, voice recordings, footage of one of the parties."

"So what happened? He got caught?"

He spread his hands and shook his head.

"The last few times I spoke to Sean, he was very worried. He was beginning to talk a bit crazy. He said he had committed a sin with a woman who was not Alicia, to try to gather information about the Vincenzo family. He was very worried because he needed absolution, and he could not go to Father O'Neil, obviously. He was also scared because he thought Father O'Neil was beginning to suspect him and Alicia. He did not know how long they had, and he said they needed to act fast, but he feared for his life and Alicia's, so he gave me a big file and told me to keep it safe, not tell him where, and if anything happened to him, to give it to the authorities. After that, he disappeared."

Dehan raised an eyebrow at him and I thought she was about to hit him.

"But you never handed the information to the authorities?"

He looked at her face for a few moments. "I am not a hero. I was quite frankly scared. There was no doubt in my mind that he and Alicia had been bumped off. I knew I could not go to the local PD, because of Michael Harragan, and I did not know how many associates he had, and to make matters worse, I knew also that one of the members of the cabal was a special agent with the FBI. I know enough, because of my specialized line of work in the law, to know how the tendrils of power spread. I honestly did not know whom to go to, to expose this thing. And so, a week became a month, became a year, became a decade, until

David tracked me down and phoned me, and told me about you."

I didn't admire him, but I understood him. Not everybody can be a Sean O'Conor, a fearless Celtic warrior.

"Who is this FBI agent?"

"I can't remember his name. Sean rarely mentioned him and he never went to the church. He was a contact of Harragan's."

Dehan glanced at me. I said to Arnav, "Where is this file now?"

"In New York, in a bank vault. The key is held by an attorney, somewhere in the United States, and if I don't contact that attorney once every six months, a copy of the file goes to the DA, and another copy to the *New York Times*."

I smiled. "You covered your bases."

"Oh yes, and there are other measures that I am not even going to tell you about."

"So, now we need to get the file to the DA without anything happening to you. How do we go about that?"

He closed his eyes and heaved a huge sigh. "I will come to New York. We will go together to the bank and we will collect the file. You can examine it there and then we will go together to the DA and hand it over, and I will make a deposition."

I thought about Bishop Bellini and his rendezvous with Dehan and me the next day at Ferry Point Park. "When?"

"The sooner the better. Tomorrow?"

I looked at Dehan. She was watching me. With Arnav's evidence, maybe I wouldn't need Bellini to incriminate himself. But I didn't know how good the evidence was, or how probative. It sounded good, but until I saw it for myself, I couldn't rely on it. I still needed Bellini red-handed. And I still needed his prints.

"Tomorrow afternoon."

He nodded. "Fine. I'll aim to be there around three. I'll go to your precinct."

I tipped my cup this way and that. It was empty and cold. "You know O'Neil is dead?"

"No, I didn't know that."

"He was executed; so was Sadiq Khan."

"Good. That man was a monster." He hesitated. "What happened to the girls?"

"They were all killed, along with Alicia, and buried in a mass grave in the churchyard."

"Oh, my God . . ."

"From what I can gather, it all happened on the same night. Your handing in this file would not have saved their lives."

"It is kind of you to say so, Detective, but I should have acted. When good men do nothing, evil prospers . . ."

I shrugged.

"Does anybody else know anything about this?"

He shook his head. "You, Detective Dehan, and me."

"Good, let's see if we can stop the body count rising any higher." But even as I said it, I knew it was a forlorn hope.

He left and we stayed, sitting in the Pavilion. It was an odd place, a latticework of green metal designed to look like a giant arbor of interlocking branches over a glade. The walls were glass, to keep you indoors while making you imagine you were outdoors. We ordered a couple of club sandwiches and a couple of beers.

While we waited, Dehan stretched back in her chair and looked at me. "So we now have one very angry Conor Hagan, who has a big beef against the Vincenzo family, and we have one bishop who is in bed with the Vincenzo family, and helped to steal one hundred grand from Hagan. I'd say Bellini has short odds on making it to the weekend."

I nodded. "We also have all the ingredients for a gang war. Conor Hagan is not a man who will back down easily, and the Vincenzos can't allow their friends to be murdered willy-nilly, it's bad for their reputation."

"But if we take him into protective custody, we blow the sting."

The sandwiches and the beer arrived, and we ate in silence.

When I'd finished, I drained my beer and sat looking at my empty plate. Eventually, I shook my head. "I am not his babysitter." I looked her in the eye. "He has the whole of the Jersey Mafia for his bodyguard. He knew what he was doing when he stole from the Irish Mob. I'm not going to blow the operation just to protect his life, so he can walk away afterwards scot-free."

She finished her sandwich without answering and then sat for a bit picking crumbs from her plate. Eventually, she nodded and said, "I agree."

I sighed. "Good."

TWENTY-FOUR

There are no benches in Ferry Point Park. It's more like a stretch of wilderness by the river that humanity hasn't destroyed yet. I was sitting on the bank, watching Dehan down on the pebbles looking out at the cold, black river. It was nine fifty. We'd had a meeting with the captain at seven a.m. and, though he was approaching the end of his tether, he also knew he had no choice but to give me what I wanted. And he had.

At three minutes past ten, Dehan turned and stared past me at the entrance to the park. Her face went hard and she said, "Not good."

I turned and looked. There was a man walking toward us. It wasn't Bishop Bellini. It was Conor Hagan. He stopped beside me, with his hands in his pockets, and looked out at the stygian water.

"Imagine meeting you two here."

I didn't say anything, and he sat next to me on the bank, studying my face.

"I figure I owe you, Stone."

"You don't owe me a goddamn thing."

"That's not for you to decide, is it? That's for me to decide."

Dehan took three or four unsteady steps over the pebbles to

stand on the moss, a couple of feet away or three. Hagan studied her a moment. She said, "Where is Bellini?"

"He's alive."

"If you feel indebted to me, Hagan, stop the killing."

He gave a lopsided smile. "You think I can stop the killing? No man, or woman, can stop the killing, Stone. You should know that."

Dehan snapped, "So you brutalize and murder Sadiq, and then Bellini, and then Vincenzo tortures and murders three of your people, and you take four of theirs, and where does it end, Conor? You have the power and the influence . . ."

"Stop." He didn't shout. He didn't even raise his voice. He said it quietly. "I have read my Kant and my Russell, and my Nietzsche, Detective Dehan, I don't need a lecture on ethics, or morality. And I am not here to discuss my actions with you. I have evaluated the situation and I have made my decisions."

"Why are you here, Hagan?"

He turned to me. "I told you, I figure I owe you a debt, and I want to pay it off."

"How?"

"These bastards stole a lot of money from me, money that I had intended to help homeless and dispossessed people, and orphaned children." He glanced at Dehan. "And before you come in with one of your wisecracks, Detective, I don't expect to be praised or admired for it. In fact, I'd rather nobody knew about it because it's bad for my image. But I actually think it's the least any man in my position should do."

He turned back to me.

"What really pisses me off is that those twisted, perverted bastards used my money to fund their sick fucking operation. Now I want my money back, and I will get it back, plus twelve years' fucking interest."

Dehan narrowed her eyes. "How are you going to do that?"

"I have something Vincenzo wants."

"The bishop."

"He knows that if he ever wants to see that little shit again in one piece—and I mean that literally—he needs to pay me back what Bellini, Sadiq, O'Neil, and Harragan stole from me."

Somewhere overhead, a seagull cried havoc and laughed. I looked at my shoes a moment.

"Okay, first, there is a name that is notably absent from your list. Second, how does any of this pay back your supposed debt?"

"You're talking about Vincenzo and Harragan's man at the bureau."

"Yeah."

"I'm coming to that. Here is how I am going to pay you back, Stone. I've arranged a meeting, at the abandoned Fish Fare warehouse on Coster Street. They give me my money, they get what's theirs returned to them. I have demanded that Vincenzo be there personally, as well as your man from the bureau. Show up, with the Seventh Cavalry, at ten p.m. tonight, not a minute before, storm the place, and you will get your prize. Show up early, Stone, and you get nothing. I guarantee it."

"I want Bellini alive, Hagan."

He spread his hands and shook his head. "You say that like I had some say in the matter. I am just giving you information, do with it as you will." He stood. "You have a good day."

And he turned and walked away across the park toward Emerson Avenue. Dehan watched him go, and when he was out of the park she said to me, "Son of a bitch! He did not incriminate himself once. Not once!"

I smiled and shook my head. "He knew one of us had a wire. Whatever Bellini told him, he knew that we were not bent and this was a sting."

"You think he's on the level?"

"In as much as a man like Hagan is ever on the level, yeah." I stood. "Let's go see Frank, then we'll go see the captain about this raid."

. . .

IT WAS A GRIM SIGHT. It's a truism, but when you're a detective in the Bronx for twenty-five years, you get to see some pretty dark things. But nothing really prepares you for seeing the skeletons of fourteen young girls, all murdered in cold blood, laid out on a table in order of size from smallest, aged eleven and twelve, to oldest, aged about twenty.

I saw Dehan waver as we stepped through the door.

"You going to be okay? You want to wait outside?"

She was pale, but she shook her head. "I'm okay."

Frank approached us across the room. He looked businesslike but glanced apologetically at Dehan.

"I'm sorry, Carmen, I know this has a personal dimension for you, but it's hard to be delicate about . . ."

"You don't need to be delicate. I'm okay."

"Sure . . . Well, first things first." He walked the length of the table, to the tallest of the skeletons. "This here is, I am afraid, your cousin, Alicia Flores."

She nodded. "I had pretty much accepted that was the case."

"We were able to determine cause of death when we put the skeleton together. The second cervical vertebra was completely shattered, and the first and third had sustained damage that was consistent with a bullet wound."

I said, "She was shot in the back of the neck."

"I think that's what I said."

"Could you determine the caliber?"

He winced. "Probably a .38."

Dehan said, "Like Sean."

Frank nodded. "But it is impossible to be more accurate than that." He pointed over at a whiteboard, where they had taped a blown-up photograph of the orphan girls from Alicia's class. "The other skeletons we have been able to match with the girls in the picture, by age and general anatomy. We are running DNA profiles on them, but of course, we have nothing to match them against as yet. It's the best we can do."

"What about cause of death?" It was Dehan. "Did they all die the same way?"

He heaved a big sigh. "The simple answer is no. In a couple, we have not been able to determine cause of death. In those cases, it was probably damage to a vital organ that did not affect the skeletal framework. In several of them, there was damage to vertebrae that was consistent with their necks being crushed, either manually, with a garrote, or even with the foot. It is impossible to be more precise. A number show lacerations on their ribs, consistent with stab wounds to the heart. There are a couple who have what are clearly gunshot wounds to the chest, again, consistent with a .38-caliber bullet."

I looked at Dehan. She was pale and her pupils were dilated. When she spoke, her voice was devoid of any emotion or feeling. "So basically, either one man set about massacring these girls in a variety of ways, or two or three people had an orgy of killing, one with his hands, another with a gun, and a third with a knife."

Frank nodded. "Yes, assuming they all died at the same time, that is correct."

I sighed. "I'll talk to the captain about organizing some kind of campaign, maybe a hotline, some TV exposure, to see if we can identify some of these girls. Some of them might have family. Somebody might remember them."

Frank nodded. "Yes. Somebody should do something to bring peace to these girls."

We left him running his DNA tests and made our way down to the parking lot. When we got there, Dehan sat on the hood of the car and stared at me.

"It wasn't just Mick, was it, Stone?"

I shook my head. "No."

"It was Sadiq and Bellini too."

"Yes."

"Why?"

"I don't know, Carmen. It was expedient. They didn't know

how much Sean and Alicia had discovered and they had to conceal the evidence."

"How can somebody do a thing like that?"

"I don't know."

"Were they high? Coke or meth?"

I shrugged. "Maybe they were just plain evil."

She was quiet for a while. "That's where he came from." She looked up at me. "That night. He was fresh from the slaughter."

I stepped forward, pulled her to me, and put my arms around her. She clung to me and started sobbing. It was convulsive, a pouring out of pain she'd held inside for twelve years, of anger and rage and impotence. We stood like that for maybe five minutes, until the storm subsided, then she stepped back and wiped her eyes on the back of her sleeves.

Some women, when they cry, look puffy and red and unattractive. Dehan was definitely one of them. Her nose was shiny and her cheeks were soaked. I pulled out a handkerchief and gave it to her. She gave a silly laugh and blew her nose in a way you could describe as anything but feminine. When she'd finished mopping her face, she hesitated and tentatively handed the handkerchief back. I smiled and shook my head. "Keep it."

She laughed. It was an oddly girly laugh, strangely out of character. "I'll wash it for you."

"I want you to take the night off, Dehan."

Her face hardened suddenly. "No way! Don't do this to me, Stone. Do not do this to me!"

I held up both hands. "Okay, if you want to come along, do. But I think this thing is too close to you. I think if you are wise, you will stay . . ."

She interrupted me. "I'm a girl! We do this kind of shit sometimes! I am fine, and you have got to let me be there at the . . ."

"At the what? At the kill?"

"I was going to say at the finish."

But we both knew she was lying.

TWENTY-FIVE

WE HAD FOUR CARS PLUS MINE, AND EIGHT OFFICERS plus myself and Dehan. We approached along Ryawa Avenue in the south and Viele in the north, without sirens. The first two cars turned down Manida Street and took up positions at the back of the warehouse. We turned down Coster Street and blockaded the exit with the cars. The windows were boarded up and the steel door was closed, but a close look showed there was no padlock on it.

I detailed two officers to stay with the cars, training their weapons on the door. The other two were to come in with Dehan and me and make the arrests. I checked my watch. It was nine fifty-five, and we waited in silence.

At exactly ten o'clock, I stepped to the door and eased it back. I expected it to wake the dead, but the rollers had been oiled and it was quiet. I opened it enough to allow us access and slipped in. Dehan followed, and then the two uniforms. We took up positions and listened.

We were in a large hangar. It was dark, but there was a soft glow coming from the back. As my eyes adjusted to the gloom, I could see that the hangar formed an *L* shape and turned right at the end. That was where the glow came from, as well as a faint murmur of voices. I gestured we should move forward, and the two uniforms headed for the wall at the angle of the *L*. Dehan was behind me, and we made for a pillar that covered the angle, and the source of the light. We were in shadow.

We crouched behind the pillar and, keeping low, I peered around. What I saw was not what I expected to see.

Vincenzo was there, in his Armani suit. He was standing. He had two of his boys with him. One of them I recognized as the Neanderthal who'd been in Sonia's office. They were standing in front of a chair. It was like a scene from a noir B movie from the fifties. There was a man tied to the chair. He looked badly bruised, but he was alive. It was Bishop Bellini.

I could see the two uniforms looking over at me, waiting for instructions. I gestured "stand by."

Alvaro Vincenzo spoke suddenly, spreading his hands in an exaggerated Italian mannerism, making funny steps with his feet. "I'm confused, Monsignor. You know, maybe you can give me some guidance. Because, you, being a bishop, you got a direct line to God, right?"

Bellini muttered something. Vincenzo ignored him.

"That's your thing, right? Everybody's got a thing in this world. Tony here, and Joe, their thing is breaking people's bones. They are really good at that, and with pliers. You like the pliers, right, Tony? Tony is real good with pliers, because pliers are like his thing.

"My thing?! My thing is making money, and keeping money. Money is my thing, Monsignor. And like Tony and Joe, I am real good at my thing."

He took a couple of steps closer to the bishop, jutting out his knees as he walked. He leaned forward so his face was close to the bishop's.

"You know why I am good, Monsignor Roberto Bellini? Because . . . because I am not stupid! Because I do not allow people to screw me! Because I am fuckin' ruthless!"

He looked back at his boys. They looked passive, as though

they were watching a TV show just because it was on, not because they were interested. Vincenzo's knees were still going, like he had a nervous condition that affected his legs, first one and then the other. His little "I am a tough guy" dance.

"Your thing is talking to God. So I am wondering . . ." He laughed an incredulous laugh. "I am wondering how come, how come, if you can talk to God, He allowed you to do something so fuckin' stupid as stealing money from me!"

I frowned at Dehan. She was frowning back. Had Hagan sold Vincenzo a line?

The Don was talking again.

"What's that? What's that? You didn't steal from me? No, no, no!" He was raising one hand. "Let's see, Monsignor, if we understand each other here, because you, and that fuckin' Mick Father O'Neil, and that other fuckin' Mick, Mick Harragan . . ." He turned, laughing, to his boys. "You see that? They're so fuckin' stupid they even call themselves Mick!" The boys laughed and he turned back to Bellini. "And that fuckin' Arab, Khan, see, you all enjoyed my protection, which you were always very happy to use when it suited you. But you see, that comes at a price. It means, you run a business, you pull a heist, you do a job, and I get my percentage. Anything, anything that goes down, I get my interest, my fuckin' consideration. And you had the fuckin' gall! You had the fuckin' affrontery! You had the fuckin' impudence to scam Conor Hagan, without my fuckin' permission, and steal one hundred fuckin' thousand dollars from me!"

With that, he gave him three powerful backhanders that echoed around the warehouse.

I turned to Dehan and nodded. Conor Hagan was a subtle and intelligent man, who should never be underestimated. I looked over at the two officers and signaled again to await my signal.

Then another voice spoke. It was deep and resonant, and familiar.

"Let's get this over with, Alvaro. I am not comfortable here. I don't even know why you called me."

I couldn't see the speaker. He seemed to be sitting on a crate behind Tony. Vincenzo turned toward him. "I told you. Hagan wants to talk to you. He's given us a gesture of goodwill; the least we can do is listen to him. He's a fuckin' Mick, but we are all Catholics. I'd rather cooperate with him than get into a fuckin' war with him."

"I'm giving him another five minutes. If he doesn't show, I am out of here."

"He'll show, if he wants his fuckin' money."

I knew in that moment that he did not plan to show and he had written off the money. He was going to recover it another way. I gave the uniforms the thumbs-up and stepped out from behind the pillar. At the same time, Dehan stepped out from the other side, and I shouted, "Freeze! NYPD! You are surrounded! Drop your weapons!"

Tony reached for his piece. I shot him in the heart and he kind of folded up and lay down. Immediately, there was an answering shot from behind Vincenzo, and one of the two uniformed cops fell. I shouted again, "Freeze!"

Dehan was shouting into her radio to the two cops I'd left at the cars, "Officer down! Officer down! Move in!"

Then, everything happened at once. Vincenzo stuck his hands up in the air, while Joe pulled his piece to fire. The other uniform screamed, "Drop it!" and the unseen shooter fired twice and dropped him. Dehan and I both fired and Joe went down. Feet were running behind us. Another shot and the light went out. Dehan was shouting, "A flashlight! A flashlight! Get back to the car! Get a flashlight!" More feet running, and for a moment there was a silhouette against the pale oblong of the open door. One of the uniforms, a crack, a spit of fire, and the silhouette cried out and fell.

Then there was stillness and absolute silence. Dehan's voice again. "Officers down! Repeat, officers down! Request immediate backup to Coster Street!"

I whispered to Dehan, "Cover me!" and sprinted headlong for the door, keeping low. I threw myself on the floor and rolled to the left of the opening. Two cracks and two whining ricochets off the steel blind. I crawled toward the opening, took a hold of the door, and heaved it back, widening the gap by about four feet. Then, I frantically scrambled and rolled over the threshold under a hail of bullets; next I was up and running for the nearest car. A movement behind me and a voice shouted, "Detective! This one!"

It was the other uniform, making for his car. As he jumped in, I said, "I'll cover you!" In the distance, I could hear the screeching of rubber on blacktop as the other cars approached. He fired up the engine, hit the gas, and, with his lights on long and a wild screaming of tires, he slammed the patrol car through the entrance. The hangar was immediately flooded with light. I followed him in and dodged to the side, into the shadows, swinging my piece left and right, searching the warehouse for the shooter.

Next thing, I was hit by an express train and slammed onto the floor. The wind was knocked out of me and instinctively I covered my head and face with my arms. They took the full brunt of a fist like a ball of rock that slammed into me twice. Then a big foot stamped on my ribs and my assailant was gone.

I staggered to my feet, feeling like somebody had rammed a crowbar through my lungs. As I went back through the door, the two cars that had been covering the back, in Manida Street, came blazing in from north and south. I winced in the glare of their headlamps, searching for my assailant. I couldn't see him. I stepped into the road, waving the cars to stop, shouting at them, "Search the road! One man! Six two! Black! In a suit!"

Then they were out of their cars, the beams from their flashlights bobbing in the darkness, probing behind the cars, under the cars, moving away from me. My mind was spinning.

I ran back to my car and called dispatch. "We have three officers down and two suspects, all injured or dead. We need ambulances. We have one escaped suspect. Request backup patrols to search the Coster Street area, black male, six two or six three, powerfully built, armed and dangerous, wearing an expensive suit." I gave them the parameters of the search, but even as I was doing it, I knew it was hopeless.

The uniforms came back at a jog. "No sign of him, Detective. What do you want us to do?"

"You two take the car, start searching west, he may have made for the park. I'll see if I can get a chopper." They scrambled for their car. I turned to the other two. "You two, get inside, assist Detective Dehan with the arrest."

They headed inside at a run and I called the captain.

"Stone, what the hell is going on?"

"Not now. You'll have my report. I need a full manhunt. I need a chopper over Barretto Park and I need every available car crawling over every inch of Hunts Point."

"Have you . . ."

"Now, Captain! Every second counts! I'm bringing Vincenzo in. We'll talk then."

"You wha . . ."

But I'd hung up, and as the sirens began to wail across the night, I went back inside. The officer who had been shot while trying to get the flashlight was on the floor, receiving first aid from his partner. The other two who had gone down in the firefight were dead. Dehan had Vincenzo in cuffs, sitting on the floor, and the two cops from the patrol car were untying Bellini. He looked rough.

The sirens swelled in volume and the pulse of red-and-blue lights filled the hangar to the screech of brakes. Next thing, paramedics were streaming in like ants and somebody was barking, "Get this damn car out of the doorway!"

I stepped over to Dehan. She was looking down at the bishop, talking to him, reading him his rights. Then the cops had him on his feet, and they were pulling his arms behind his back. His face was ugly and swollen. One eye was completely closed and the other swiveled, looking at me with pure, undiluted hatred. And in that moment, he keeled over and fell.

He sprawled in a heap next to Tony's lifeless body. One of the cops shouted, "Paramedic! We need a paramedic here!"

Then everything happened in slow motion. I could see his eye, still focused on me. I could see Dehan, looking down at him, taking half a step back. One cop was shouting, looking for the ambulance teams, the other was bending to assist Bellini. And Bellini's right hand was reaching, reaching out for Tony's automatic. He swung it around in a slow arc till it was leveled straight at my chest. I was aware my legs ached, my head was foggy, and I had shooting pains like blades in my chest. I knew I had to move, but I knew I was going to be too slow.

There was a noise like two doors slamming in rapid succession. Bellini was still staring at me. His gun was trained on me. He seemed to convulse and gurgle, and blood spewed from his mouth. There was a big, ugly hole in his chest. He lay back and died. I turned and looked at Dehan. She was staring at Bellini and she was holding her automatic in both hands.

She turned to me. "Are you okay?"

"I'm not sure. How many rounds did you pull off?"

"Two."

I nodded. "Then I'm okay."

"Detective?"

I turned. There was a paramedic looking up at me, frowning. She was pretty and I smiled at her. "Hi."

"You're bleeding. Quite a lot."

TWENTY-SIX

"WE HAVE TO GET YOU TO THE HOSPITAL, DETECTIVE."

"No, what you have to do is give me something for the pain, plug the hole, and let me do my job."

I was sitting in the back of an ambulance with my shirt off, a drip in my arm and the pretty paramedic examining a hole in my shoulder. Overhead, I could hear the thud of the chopper searching Barretto Point. I was watching Vincenzo being loaded in the back of a patrol car and the dead cops being wheeled out on gurneys and loaded into the back of a meat wagon. Dehan was staring at me.

"Don't be an ass, Stone."

"I yam what I yam and dat's what I yam."

She sighed. I made a "whatcha gonna do?" face.

The pretty paramedic said, "You were lucky, Detective, it's a through and through. Couple of inches down and it would have punctured your lung. Even so, you need to get to a hospital."

I smiled at her. "It means a lot to me that you care. Put a plaster on it and I promise to go to the hospital tomorrow, first thing, after breakfast."

She sighed and started patching me up. Dehan was shaking her head. I noticed the way the red-and-blue lights washed the planes of her face and her cheekbones and realized I was still a little high on shock. A car pulled up and the captain climbed out. He had a look of outrage on his face.

"What in the name of . . . ?"

Dehan cut across him with a voice like frozen hydrogen fashioned into a blade.

"Detective Stone was injured in the line of duty, sir! He was shot while attempting to save myself and other officers!"

He frowned at her a moment, then looked at me. "Is it serious?"

"Just a graze."

The pretty paramedic had to speak up. "It is not just a graze! It is a gunshot wound and needs proper medical attention at the hospital."

"Stone, you are to go to the hospital and have that wound seen to, then I want a report on my desk."

I smiled at the paramedic. I said sweetly, "Don't talk." Then I smiled at the captain. "Captain, I will do that, but we are not done, and I cannot afford the time to do that right now. There are things you need to know." I was aware I was not speaking normally.

Dehan opened her mouth, and I gave her a look that Julius Caesar might have given Brutus seconds before he stabbed him. She closed her mouth, the Captain didn't.

"Detective, I am giving you . . ."

I interrupted him. "Please don't make me disobey a direct order, Captain. It would look so bad on TV and in the papers. Especially when they report the bent FBI agent angle."

His open mouth sagged, then closed. "I hope you know what you are doing, John."

"That is a wish we share, John. Now, with your permission, I need to go and talk to Mr. Alvaro Vincenzo."

I turned to the paramedic. "Did anybody ever tell you you are real pretty?"

She gave me "that look" and said, "Yeah, my mom. Did

anybody ever tell you you're a real ass? Oh, yeah, your partner, who knows you best. Put this on."

She looked past me and winked at Dehan, then slipped a sling over my neck and fitted my arm in it. I gave Dehan the keys to my Jag and said, "To the station, Detective."

A dull, penetrating ache had started in my shoulder and was sending the occasional needle into my back and lungs. I ignored them and put my hand on the captain's shoulder. "The man we are hunting for, Captain, is Special Agent Paul Harrison, and I have got to be in at the kill. You understand that, right?"

He followed me to the car, gripping my arm, trying to pull me back. "What the hell are you talking about? Who the hell is Special Agent Paul Harrison?"

"He was the liaison between the Feds, Vincenzo, and Pro, Maurice Learner, Vincenzo's top hit man."

"And what in the name of all that is holy, Stone, has he got to do with this?"

I opened the door to the passenger seat and heard the reassuring growl of the Jaguar firing up.

"I'll fill you in at the station, Captain."

We eased out of Coster Street and onto Viele Avenue. I slid back in the seat and gave myself a few seconds to indulge in shameless suffering. Dehan's voice invaded my pain.

"I am this close to taking you to the hospital."

I spoke without opening my eyes. "If you do, I will never be your date again. I'm fine, just give me a second, talk me through it."

She sighed noisily.

"You were right, as usual, 'H' was Harrison. But he and Bellini were working behind Vincenzo's back, using Father O'Neil to steal money from Conor Hagan, playing on his twisted ethics about serving his community."

"A fact," I said, wincing as a four-foot shard of glass stabbed through my right lung, "that Conor Hagan learned from Bellini, probably under torture, and exploited with some skill tonight."

We joined the Bruckner Expressway and she began to accelerate.

"Yeah, he wrote off his hundred grand, or figured it was a fair price to pay to get the Italian Mob off his turf. What I am not clear about is whether he knew about Harrison."

I nodded. "He indicated as much when we talked to him at the Shamrock, and it was him who insisted he should be there tonight."

"Right, his payback to you for revealing Father O'Neil's scam to him, but what I don't get is how he could have known about Harrison."

Maybe the pretty paramedic had given me a painkiller. The pain was subsiding, and I was getting an agreeable floating sensation, like my body was drifting away from me. I smiled.

"Remember when we were hunting for Harragan? The Nelson Hernandez case? The original investigating officer in that case put us onto Special Agent Harrison as a way of contacting Pro, Vincenzo's hit man, remember?"

"Of course, he was in witness protection."

"Right. Pro and Mick were tight, because Mick facilitated the Jersey Mob's operations in the Bronx. Harrison was Pro and Vincenzo's man in the bureau."

"Okay, I get all that, but . . ."

"Well, Dehan, Mick was also Hagan's facilitator, probably more so than anybody else's, because they were both Irish. Mick would have bragged to Hagan about his man in the bureau. Hagan would have known all about him."

She nodded. "Of course."

"So he handed us Vincenzo and his man in the FBI, as an act of enlightened self-interest. He pays me back and at the same time gets the Italians out of his manor."

We pulled up outside the precinct and she killed the engine. She sat looking at me like an angry mother. I tried not to snicker.

"I think she gave you morphine."

"You should always have some in your kitchen cupboard."

"You're in no state to conduct an interrogation, Stone."

I held up two fingers. "Just one question, Dehan, then you can take me home and mother me. But if ever you have trusted my judgment, trust it now."

She got out and slammed the door, then helped me out and we walked together to the station house.

Vincenzo was in interrogation room six. When Dehan and I walked in, he pointed at me like his finger was a revolver and I half expected him to say, "Bang! Bang!" Instead, he said, "I ain't sayin' nothin' to you until my lawyer gets here. Murder! Murder of a bishop! Attempted murder! I am going to have your job, Stone! I am going to have your fuckin' ass!"

I sat down and regarded him with a feeling of peace and goodwill that was entirely chemical.

"I can't blame you for the way you feel, Alvaro. Anyone in your position would feel the same, I am sure."

Dehan put her hand to her brow and discreetly covered her eyes. I managed to repress an inappropriate chuckle. It may even have been a giggle. I knew I had a very few minutes before I had to go somewhere and sleep.

"Just tell me something, Alvaro, because in the morning I am going to be thinking in terms of whether I can cut you a deal. I couldn't see clearly—was it you who fired the shot that killed the officer, or was it Paul Harrison?"

"It was Paul. I didn't fire a shot. It was Paul."

"Thank you." I stood. "I just wanted to confirm that Paul Harrison was there." I turned to the uniform by the door. "You can put him in the cell now."

He scowled at me as we left.

My legs were turning into anacondas as Dehan helped me down the stairs and into my car. As she climbed in next to me, I said, "Take me home, baby." And after that, darkness enfolded me.

TWENTY-SEVEN

THE SUN WAS BRIGHT, TOO BRIGHT. MY SHOULDER hurt, but I no longer felt high, or like giggling. Good smells of coffee and bacon, now inextricably linked with Dehan for all time, came to me from the kitchen. I was on the sofa, dressed. I raised myself on my good elbow, which meant I was uncomfortably facing the back of the sofa.

"What time is it?"

"Time you got up and had a doctor look at your dressing."

"You done the first aid course?"

A sigh audible over the sizzling of bacon. "Yes . . ."

"You can do it. What time is it?"

"Ten."

"Shit!"

I swung my legs off the sofa and suffered in silence for a few seconds. When the pain subsided, I said, "We need to interrogate Vincenzo. And Singh is coming at three."

She carried the pan to the table and started putting bacon on the plates.

"You'll interrogate, but first you'll eat. The captain called."

I stood. "Did they find Harrison?"

"Uh-uh."

"Dammit!"

"But now the bureau is hunting for him nationwide. They are embarrassed."

"Damn right. They should be."

I walked gingerly to the kitchen and sat. I tried removing my right arm from the sling but my shoulder told me that was a bad idea by setting fire to my arm. I made small gasping noises. Dehan put two eggs on my plate, then sat opposite and took my plate away from me. I watched her cut my toast, my eggs, and my bacon into small, manageable pieces, then she put the plate in front of me again and put my fork in my left hand.

"Can you manage, or you want me to feed you?"

"I can manage."

She started to tuck in with her usual enthusiasm and vigor. "So explain something to me."

"What?"

"Why the big to-do last night? You had to ask Vincenzo one question! Just one question! Who shot the cop, him or Harrison? We both saw clear as daylight who shot the cop."

"Oh, that."

"What? Oh, that? What?"

"Did you see Paul Harrison at any point?"

"No, but I assumed you did when he attacked you at the door."

"Uh-uh. I didn't see him. I thought I recognized his voice, but I wasn't sure."

"You told the captain . . ."

I shrugged. "I'm pretty sure it was him, and I wanted the captain motivated in his manhunt. I figured he would be more motivated hunting a mole in the FBI than just a Mafia goon. But I couldn't swear in court that it was Harrison. So I thought I'd cover my bases."

"So you asked Vincenzo a fake question . . ."

"So he would confirm Harrison was there. Yup."

She ate in silence for a bit and drank her coffee while I struggled left-handed. Then, she said, "Vincenzo lawyered up and he says he wants a deal."

"What did the captain say?"

"He says he wants to know your opinion. Vincenzo says he can give us the New Jersey family, plus new evidence to convict Pro, and Harrison."

"We already got Harrison." I shrugged. "Let's see what Sean had, then we can talk to Vincenzo about a deal."

ARNAV SINGH WAS as good as his word. He arrived at the precinct at ten to three. I had arrived there with Dehan at twelve and been debriefed by the captain. We had discussed how to approach a deal with Vincenzo and, after much talk, reached the conclusion I had already reached that morning over breakfast. That we should first see what evidence Sean had collected.

We didn't waste time. Singh had the key to the bank deposit box and we took my car. Dehan drove. The United Commercial Bank was on the corner of Fletcher Street and Pearl. We found space to park on John Street around the corner and walked the hundred yards to the bank.

Inside, we crossed the cold, green marble floor under cavernous, echoing ceilings to a highly polished desk, where Singh showed a card and his ID to a nervous man who kept pushing eyeglasses that were too heavy back up a nose that was too short.

"I'd like to withdraw the contents of this box."

"Of course, please follow me."

He led us through a security door, down a long, carpeted passage, through another security door into an anteroom, and finally into a concrete vault with ranks of impregnable steel boxes. The clerk identified the box in question and discreetly stepped outside to wait.

Singh opened the box and pulled out a blue file that was at least four inches thick. He placed it on a table and opened it.

"I know he was ready to go to the cops, or to the Feds. His

only worry was that he knew Father O'Neil had bent connections, but I think what he collected here will be enough for a conviction."

I glanced at Dehan. I knew she was thinking the same as me: there was practically nobody left to convict. Just Harrison, and he had only been marginally involved. I leafed through it. There were more pictures of the girls, others of boys. There were copies of bank statements, emails, telephone records with numbers highlighted, CDs, and DVDs. It was too much to take in, but it looked detailed. Very detailed.

I nodded at Singh. "It looks good. I need to go through it in detail, but it looks good, Singh. Thanks for coming forward."

He sighed and shook his head. "It will be a relief to put it behind me. It has been a weight on my conscience for all these years. What I will never be able to shake is the fact that I didn't act sooner."

Dehan picked up the file. "We were all too late to save the kids, Singh. At least now we can lay them to rest in peace, and close the case."

"Yuh, thanks."

The clerk led us back along the carpeted corridor and out into the vast, echoing marble hall. Singh pushed his way through the revolving glass doors. Dehan was just behind him. I watched him come out onto the sidewalk and stop to wait for her as I pushed with my left hand. Through the glass, I saw Paul Harrison jogging across the road, through the traffic. Dehan hadn't seen him. I shouted, but the glass was too thick and she didn't hear. I roared and heaved with all my weight, but it was like I was pushing through cold treacle.

Dehan looked at him as he came up on the sidewalk. He stuck out his arm, rigid and straight. He had a silenced 9mm Sig Sauer 226 in his hand. It bucked twice and a plume of blood erupted from Arnav's head. It was just a couple of seconds. I was still screaming and heaving on the door. I watched as his rigid arm swung round. I saw the perfect black circle of the muzzle pointing directly at Dehan's head. I saw the file fall to the sidewalk, and then Dehan moved like a striking viper.

Her left hand had the muzzle of the automatic. Her right smashed into his wrist and she levered the gun out of his fingers. In less than a second, he was disarmed. Her right foot lashed out in a blinding kick, but he was already dodging, dropping.

As I exploded from the revolving doors, he was scooping up the file and running, half stumbling, weaving through the crowds. Dehan was screaming, "Freeze! Stop! Stop!" But there was no way she could shoot in the crowded street. I didn't pause. I ripped off my sling as I ran and bolted after him, shouting, "Call for backup!"

He was ten years younger than me, and an athlete, plus he was pretty much running for his life. I was ten years older, bruised and injured, and my lungs were threatening to explode, but I would be damned sooner than see him get away. Also, the crowds were not allowing him to get into his stride.

He dodged into John Street and bolted across the road. Brakes squealed and angry drivers bellowed at him. I stayed with him as he ran into Front Street and headed for the covered market. He plowed through the terraced cafés there, sending deck chairs and tables flying. It slowed him down, but my lungs were screaming, and I knew I couldn't keep going much longer.

He was just turning the corner to sprint toward Beekman Street and I was asking myself where the hell Dehan and her backup were, when a blur flashed past my left shoulder and I saw Dehan, doing an Olympic sprint, streak across the corner and launch herself into a flying tackle. She flung her arms around his legs, like they were a long-lost lover, and he slammed face-first into the sidewalk. The file skidded ahead of him and I hobbled after it.

She got to her feet and stuck the Sig against his head.

"Get up, you motherfucker!" She was panting hard and her face was flushed. He slowly got up, his nose gushing blood. He turned to look at her. He was out of breath too, but not much.

A Black Audi 8 came around the corner at speed and skidded

to a halt. The back door flew open, but nobody got out. Harrison didn't say anything. He just looked at Dehan, and walked toward the car. She looked stunned.

"Freeze!"

"It had two rounds in it. You're empty." He climbed in the car and closed the door. It took off at speed.

"What the fuck?" She looked at me. "What the fuck, Stone?"

I held up the file.

"He has friends in high places, and he is obviously still useful to somebody, but we have the file. Come on. Let's go close this goddamn case."

EPILOGUE

SHE HAD HER HAIR TIED IN A KNOT BEHIND HER HEAD. She had her sleeves rolled up above her elbows and she was perspiring. She had finished turning over the soil and was now making holes about four inches across, five or six inches deep. The sun was warm, but gentle, declining in the west toward a sweet, mid-April evening. The church was closed, pending the naming of a new priest, but the parish had given us permission to dedicate a garden to the children.

Dehan had had the sign made, and she'd brought along her own masonry drill to fix it to the church wall. It was in brass so, as she said, it would never fade and never be forgotten. It said simply, *The Garden of the Orphaned Children.* Now she was planting flowers and small trees. She had twenty-four of them, two for each child who had been buried there. I had offered to help, one-handed, but she had refused. It was something, she said, she had to do herself. I guess I understood.

She was on her knees now, with the evening sun on her, and a few strands of hair falling across her face, pressing the earth around a small rosebush.

"Your job," she said, "when I have finished, is to take me on a date, to eat a damn good steak that I can get intense about."

"You expect me to do that one-handed?"

"You're such a wimp. Here, hand me those azaleas."

I passed them over to her. She was quiet while she set the small bush in the ground and packed it with dirt. Then, she said, "Will we ever get Harrison?"

"I don't know. I'll never stop trying, but I think the bureau have a better chance than us. He could be anywhere."

She nodded. "A strange case, Stone. Did we solve it? Did we close it? The only survivor got away. All the others died, but nobody was brought to justice."

I shrugged. "What can I tell you, I'm not one for philosophizing, Carmen, but sometimes life has a justice all its own. Our justice is just overlaid, on top of it."

She made a face, reached out her hand, and said, "The orange tree." I handed it over and she went on, "You talking about a god?"

"No." I thought about it a moment, then said, "It just seems sometimes that things have a way of working out. Not always, but sometimes, it works out right."

She still didn't look at me, but she smiled. She stood and dusted the soil from her hands, then wiped them on her jeans, looking down at the small garden. "There," she said. "Give it a couple of weeks, it will look nice."

"It's beautiful."

She linked her arm through mine and we stood in silence for a minute, then she gathered up her things and we walked slowly back toward the car. She put her stuff in the trunk, and as I closed it, she said, "Did we do the right thing?"

I rested my ass against the old Jaguar and gingerly crossed my arms. "If we'd cut a deal with Vincenzo, sure, we would have trawled up ten or twenty of his lieutenants, maybe even a few people from the Manhattan Families. We'll never know. But the man responsible, the man who made the decisions, would have lived the rest of his life in comfort, like Pro, without ever paying for what he did, keeping his hand in here and there. I couldn't rest easy with that. We'll get the others, in time." I shook my head. "We can't catch everybody, but those we do catch, let's make them pay."

She nodded. "Okay. Answer me something, who killed Father O'Neil? I'm still not clear about that."

"It wasn't Vincenzo. He didn't know yet that Father O'Neil had screwed him, and it wasn't Hagan for the same reason. It had to be Bellini. When we started digging up his churchyard, word got to Bellini of what was happening, and he sent somebody to silence him. Maybe he called on Vincenzo for a couple of hit men. I guess we may never find out for sure."

She nodded. "And how did Harrison know about the file? Arnav said we were the only people who knew about that."

I wondered about that. Then I realized, when Mick killed Sean, Harrison must have burgled his house and wiped his computer. "There must have been a reference in his diary, or his papers, to the file he gave Arnav."

"Do you think Sean died here, in this church?"

I nodded. "I think so. He died on his knees. The only way I can see that happening is if he was praying. Mick shot him while he was in prayer, dressed him as a vagrant, knowing he could make the case go cold that way, and threw him in the dumpster. Then he and Khan and Bellini murdered the girls."

She was silent awhile. "I guess so. A strange case," she said again, and then, looking back into the churchyard, "We dug up the garden of the damned, and replanted it with oranges and azaleas."

"Come on, Carmen, let's get you cleaned up and go get that steak. And then maybe a few tequilas, purely for their medicinal effect, you understand."

She pulled out the keys to my car from her pocket and said, "Oh, I can use some of that medicine, Stone. I can use some of that medicine!"

And we drove away, across the dark river, leaving the garden of the damned behind us, thinking now of good food, good wine, and home.

Don't miss LET US PREY. The riveting sequel in the Dead Cold Mystery series.

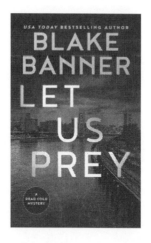

Scan the QR code below to purchase LET US PREY.

Or go to: righthouse.com/let-us-prey

NOTE: flip to the very end to read an exclusive sneak peak...

DON'T MISS ANYTHING!

If you want to stay up to date on all new releases in this series, with this author, or with any of our new deals, you can do so by joining our newsletters below.

In addition, you will immediately gain access to our entire *Right House VIP Library,* which includes many riveting Mystery and Thriller novels for your enjoyment!

righthouse.com/email

(Easy to unsubscribe. No spam. Ever.)

ALSO BY BLAKE BANNER

Up to date books can be found at:
www.righthouse.com/blake-banner

ROGUE THRILLERS
Gates of Hell (Book 1)
Hell's Fury (Book 2)

ALEX MASON THRILLERS
Odin (Book 1)
Ice Cold Spy (Book 2)
Mason's Law (Book 3)
Assets and Liabilities (Book 4)
Russian Roulette (Book 5)
Executive Order (Book 6)
Dead Man Talking (Book 7)
All The King's Men (Book 8)
Flashpoint (Book 9)
Brotherhood of the Goat (Book 10)
Dead Hot (Book 11)
Blood on Megiddo (Book 12)
Son of Hell (Book 13)

HARRY BAUER THRILLER SERIES
Dead of Night (Book 1)
Dying Breath (Book 2)
The Einstaat Brief (Book 3)
Quantum Kill (Book 4)
Immortal Hate (Book 5)
The Silent Blade (Book 6)
LA: Wild Justice (Book 7)

Breath of Hell (Book 8)
Invisible Evil (Book 9)
The Shadow of Ukupacha (Book 10)
Sweet Razor Cut (Book 11)
Blood of the Innocent (Book 12)
Blood on Balthazar (Book 13)
Simple Kill (Book 14)
Riding The Devil (Book 15)
The Unavenged (Book 16)
The Devil's Vengeance (Book 17)
Bloody Retribution (Book 18)
Rogue Kill (Book 19)
Blood for Blood (Book 20)

DEAD COLD MYSTERY SERIES
An Ace and a Pair (Book 1)
Two Bare Arms (Book 2)
Garden of the Damned (Book 3)
Let Us Prey (Book 4)
The Sins of the Father (Book 5)
Strange and Sinister Path (Book 6)
The Heart to Kill (Book 7)
Unnatural Murder (Book 8)
Fire from Heaven (Book 9)
To Kill Upon A Kiss (Book 10)
Murder Most Scottish (Book 11)
The Butcher of Whitechapel (Book 12)
Little Dead Riding Hood (Book 13)
Trick or Treat (Book 14)
Blood Into Wine (Book 15)
Jack In The Box (Book 16)
The Fall Moon (Book 17)
Blood In Babylon (Book 18)
Death In Dexter (Book 19)
Mustang Sally (Book 20)

ABOUT US

Right House is an independent publisher created by authors for readers. We specialize in Action, Thriller, Mystery, and Crime novels.

If you enjoyed this novel, then there is a good chance you will like what else we have to offer! Please stay up to date by using any of the links below.

Join our mailing lists to stay up to date --> righthouse.com/email
Visit our website --> righthouse.com
Contact us --> contact@righthouse.com

 facebook.com/righthousebooks

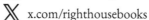 x.com/righthousebooks

 instagram.com/righthousebooks

EXCLUSIVE SNEAK PEAK OF...

LET US PREY

CHAPTER 1

EVEN THE MAD DOGS WERE PANTING IN THE SHADE, AND the Englishmen were mopping their brows and sipping G&Ts. There was a fly on my desk that I was sure had died of heat exhaustion a couple of hours earlier. Every now and then, the electric fan ruffled its wings, but that was all the movement it was capable of. The technicians who'd come in to fix the air-conditioning were too hot to work, so we were trapped in a negative spiral of heat and eventual death by dehydration.

Dehan, who had her boots on the desk and her hair tied in a knot behind her head to keep her neck cool, said, "Edgar Gonzalez, known member of the Chupa Cabra gang, shot down in a drive-by outside his parents' house on Irvine Street."

She tossed it in the "not now not ever" box. We had unofficially established the criteria for investigating a case as a) having some remote chance of being solved, and b) that the crime was not itself a positive benefit to humanity as a whole.

I said, "Clive Henderson, on holiday from California, mugged and stabbed on Commonwealth Avenue." I put it in the "maybe" pile. In this weather, a trip to California was appealing, even though the case hadn't an ice cube's chance in a supernova of ever being solved.

"So, what's the deal with you, Stone?"

Dehan was leafing through another file. I reached for one and settled back to read it. I had no intention of answering a question like that, but she persisted.

"You ever been married? You got a long string of exes? You gay? What gives? Why do I never see you with a woman?"

I made my eyebrows climb my forehead. "Why do you want to know?"

"C'mon. We're partners. I told you all about me. It's your turn."

I sighed. "Meth dealer shot outside the fish market on Food Center Drive." I threw the file in the "not now not ever" pile. It satisfied both criteria. "I was married," I said. "Seven years. It was enough."

She studied me a moment, then carried on reading. "How long ago?"

"Five years."

"Do you date?"

I sighed more loudly and said, "Yeah, I date this babe—she's a lot younger than me, but she has a filthy attitude and she's too nosy."

She chuckled, and the internal phone rang. I picked it up.

"Stone."

"Good afternoon, Stone, it's the captain. Will you and Detective Dehan please come to my office?"

I hung up. "Come on, Nosy, get your butt out of that chair—the captain wants us."

We climbed the stairs, mopping sweat from our brows, and knocked on his door. He told us to go in, and we did. His window was open, letting all the warm air in.

"It's not the heat," he said as we sat down. "It's the humidity." I'd never heard anybody say that before. As I drew breath to make a wisecrack, he said, "Have you ever heard of Karl Baxter?"

I shook my head. "Nope."

Dehan echoed my shake. "No, sir."

"He's a private investigator, operates out of an office on Melrose Avenue." He pulled a face and made a "so-so" gesture with his hand. "Moderately successful because he's not too scrupulous about the kind of cases he takes. I've been looking into his background because he called me today to ask to have sight of a file on one of our cold cases."

I frowned. "Has he turned bounty hunter?"

The captain shook his head. "No, there is no reward on this case."

Dehan went straight to the point. "What's the case?"

"Stephen Springfellow. Shot to death in his apartment on 155th Street. As usual, lack of forensic evidence and witnesses led to the case going cold."

"We'll have a look at the file and have a chat with Baxter. I'd like to know why he's interested in the case."

"Precisely. Whether it's a personal interest, or a client's interest, it could shed light on the murder." He pushed a sheet of paper across the desk. I reached for it. It was Baxter's address. "Normally does 'wife watching'"—he made the quotation marks sign with his fingers—"but he has been known to track down missing persons who were trying to keep a low profile. They have somehow tended to wind up in hospital or in the river after he finds them. Not that he does the hit; he's just the finder. And gets a finder's fee."

Dehan raised an eyebrow. "A rat."

He looked at her and smiled. "Yes, Detective Dehan, but try not to beat him up or terrorize him. We need his cooperation."

She smiled back. "Who, me?"

He chuckled without much humor. "All right, Detectives, go and see what you can find out."

Back downstairs, Dehan found the file in the box. She dropped into her chair and started reading, while I stood in front of the fan.

"Stephen Springfellow, white male, thirty-two, found shot through the heart in his apartment on East 155th Street on

June 14, 2015." She pulled a happy face and glanced at me. "Recent. Makes a change. He was tied to a chair and had been badly beaten. He had his wallet in his back pocket with a hundred bucks in it, plus his credit card, ID, and driver's license. Nothing appeared to be missing from his apartment. The lock had not been forced. The neighbors heard nothing, except that the one who called it in heard two gunshots close together and reported seeing a couple of members of the Sureños gang nearby. However, she then refused to make an official statement, and in any case, it was not enough to make an arrest."

She pulled out some photographs of the crime scene and spread them on the desk. They showed a small, seedy apartment with an unmade bed, a table with three chairs around it, and a small, open-plan kitchen. Near the table, Stephen Springfellow was sprawled over the fourth chair. His ankles were tied to the chair legs, and his hands were tied behind the backrest. His face was badly bruised and swollen, and the front of his shirt was drenched and clotted with blood that was beginning to dry. You could see the dark circle of the entry wound to the right—his left —of his sternum.

I sat, pulled one of the pictures over to me, and started to examine it. Dehan was leafing through the file.

"He had previous. He was a small-time crook. Burglary, petty theft, brawls, but nothing major. Spent a couple of years in San Francisco, came back east 2014."

"Maybe he was trying for the next level, wanted to play with the big boys." I said it absently because something in the picture had caught my eye.

Dehan grunted. "Maybe. He obviously got the wrong people pissed. One slug was recovered. It was a .38."

"What does it say about the blood on the floor?"

She looked at the photograph and frowned. "Huh!" She read for a bit, then said, "Blood on the floor, about two feet in front of the victim, possibly consistent with a second victim, though no other victim was found at the apartment or in the vicinity. So they looked."

I stared at her. "*Possibly* consistent with another victim? That's what it says?"

"Yup." She tossed the file across to me and started examining the photographs.

I read again. "Nobody heard anything, except the neighbor who called it in. Saw some Sureños . . . then heard two shots close together . . ." I looked up at her. "Two shots."

She sat back. "Okay. So he decides he wants to move into the big leagues. He partners up with some tough guy, does a job that steps on the Sureños' toes. They get pissed, pay him a visit, and ice him . . ."

"Ice him? You been reading Mickey Spillane?"

"Of course. Questions: Who is this tough guy? Why did they leave Stephen but take away the second victim? Where is the second victim now?"

I leaned back. "Speculation: Did the second victim come up with the information that they were trying to beat out of Stephen?"

"So Stephen was no longer of any use. They iced him and took away victim two."

I nodded. "It's possible."

I picked up the phone and dialed. It rang twice and a voice on the other end said, "Baxter, private investigator. How may I help you?"

"Mr. Baxter, this is Detective Stone of the NYPD. You wanted to have sight of one of our files."

"Ah, Detective Stone, yes indeed. Good of you to call back. The Stephen Springfellow case."

"We would like to talk to you about that. Are you available this afternoon?"

There was a smile in his voice. "I rather imagined you would, Detective. Yes, come right on over. Six eighty Melrose Avenue, over the African hair-braiding salon."

"We'll be there in twenty minutes."

CHAPTER 2

OUTSIDE, A HARSH GLARE WAS ADDED TO THE relentless, humid heat. The streets were practically empty, and the plane trees across the road looked depressed. My Jag, a burgundy 1964 Mark II, was like an oven. The steering wheel was almost too hot to hold. I smiled—at least we had working air-conditioning.

As we accelerated down the Bruckner Expressway, luxuriating in the cold air from the dash, I said, "The other question, Dehan, is what is the connection between Baxter's client and the victim or victims?"

"Yeah, I was making a mental list." She held up her thumb. "Client is seeking revenge. Could be a husband, wife, son, daughter, sister, brother. So we should have a look at Stephen's close relationships."

She held up her index finger. I glanced at it and was struck by the fact that it was long and slender, like a pianist's finger. "Or it could be another kind of revenge . . ."

"Professional, as of a gang, a mob . . . something of that sort."

"Yeah, or three"—she held up thumb, index, and middle finger—"Baxter's client is looking for whatever Stephen's killers were looking for. Whether that is information or an actual, physical object, we don't know. And of course, all of this applies to

Stephen's co-victim. It's possible Baxter's client has no interest whatsoever in Stephen."

"Mm-hm." I nodded. "The fact that the second victim was removed from the apartment suggests that he, or she, was of interest to the killers. How do we feel about the Sureños?"

She shrugged. "They were probably there, but then, they are everywhere. It's a bit early to say."

I had pulled off onto East 163rd and was headed west toward Morrisania.

"He won't want to tell us who his client is, and he doesn't have to. But he's ready to trade something, or he wouldn't have invited us to go see him."

Ten minutes later, I pulled up across the road from the African hairstylist. The hot air as we climbed out of the Jag was like a furnace blast. We dodged through the traffic and buzzed at the door. The door opened and we stepped into the relative cool of the lobby. An old-fashioned elevator with concertina doors carried us to the fourth floor. Baxter's was the second door down. It had a frosted glass pane with his name on it in gold letters, like in the movies. We knocked and went in. There was no gorgeous secretary, but I guess you can't have everything.

He stood as we came in and approached us smiling, with his hand stuck out.

"Karl Baxter. Thanks so much for taking the trouble to come and see me."

We shook and showed him our badges. He glanced at them as he ushered us toward two chairs across from his desk. He was no Philip Marlowe or Sam Spade, more the Continental Op. He was short, maybe five five, with balding, black hair and horn-rimmed glasses. He was perspiring, his belly was becoming a paunch, and he hadn't shaved that morning. He was nervous too, of a nervous disposition.

We sat and declined coffee. There was a fan in the corner blowing warm air around the room and occasionally ruffling the papers on his desk. When he'd finally sat down, I smiled at him and asked, "Mr. Baxter, what is your interest in the Stephen Springfellow case?"

He hesitated a moment, like he had several lies lined up and hadn't decided which one to use yet. In the end, he plumbed for, "As a matter of fact, I am writing a book on cold cases."

Dehan raised an eyebrow. "You reckon you can get a whole paragraph out of that case?"

His cheeks colored. "It has some interesting features."

"Like?"

He smiled nervously. He was obviously wishing he'd gone with one of his other lies. I offered him a tolerant smile.

"How about we start again, and this time you tell us the truth? I am not opposed in principle to letting you see the file, Mr. Baxter, but please, don't insult our intelligence." I shrugged. "And play ball with us; we'll play back."

He looked embarrassed. "I apologize. My client insists on the utmost discretion . . ."

"I understand. Can you tell us who your client is?"

"Out of the question."

"What can you tell us?"

He sighed deeply and made a big show of looking reluctant. "You may not be aware of this, Detectives, but besides Springfellow and his killer, or killers, there was somebody else in the apartment."

I looked skeptical and glanced at Dehan. She made a "yeah, right" face. "What makes you say so?"

"If you examine the photographs—refer to the ones that were published in the press—you'll see there is a patch of blood that does not belong to Springfellow."

I shrugged. "So Springfellow cut one of his attackers before they subdued him and tied him to the chair."

He smiled and blinked a few times. "No, Detective, there was somebody else in the room."

"How do you know?"

"I am not at liberty to tell you that."

Dehan sighed loudly and looked as though she was about to stand and leave. "You're blowing smoke, Baxter. We've gone to the trouble of coming here, and we are willing to cooperate with you. But you've got to do better than, 'There was somebody else in the room.' That's bullshit and you know it."

I gave him a bland smile and said, "I might express myself differently, Baxter, but my sentiments are the same. You are wasting our time and your own."

I made to stand.

"Wait."

I paused and looked at him.

"I can tell you who was there."

I sat. "You mean you know who the killer was?"

"No. I don't. I mean I can tell you who *else* was there."

"The other victim?"

"The other person who was present, besides Stephen Springfellow and his killers, was a woman. Her name was Tamara Gunthersen—Tammy. She disappeared and has never been seen or heard of again."

"And this is who your client is looking for?"

"I am not at liberty to tell you that, Detective." He shrugged and smiled. "But if you draw that conclusion, I can't stop you. Now . . . do I get to look at the file?"

I'd brought it with me, and it was sitting on my lap. I dropped it on the desk in front of him. "I made a copy for you. There isn't a lot in it. You understand that any information you uncover that is, or could be, relevant to a criminal investigation, you are obliged to share with us."

"I am aware of that, Detective."

Dehan said, "In that case, Baxter, can you tell us what Tammy was doing at Stephen's house, and what interest his killers could have had in her? Why would they remove her body, or indeed kill her, in the first place?"

He spread his hands. "I don't know. That is what I have been hired to find out. That really is all I know." He gestured with both hands at the file. "Why else would I be asking you for this file?"

I nodded. He had a point. "What else can you tell me about Tamara Gunthersen? You must know something about her."

"I can tell you she was born in San Francisco on January 5, 1993. And that really is all I can tell you for now. You have my word that as soon as I unearth any more information, you will be the first"—he gave an ingratiating smile—"perhaps the second, to know."

"We appreciate it, Baxter."

Back down in the searing glare of the afternoon sun, I climbed in behind the wheel, and Dehan put the air-con on. I fired up the engine, and we started back toward the 43rd.

"I don't know about you, Dehan, but I am having trouble visualizing this whole situation."

She nodded. "Yup, me too."

"Talk me through it."

"Okay, here is Steve the yegg . . ."

"Yegg?" I laughed. "You have been reading Mickey Spillane."

"I love Mickey Spillane. So here is Steve, a small-time yegg. He's in his apartment. Maybe Tammy is there with him, over from Frisco for some reason." I smiled at her, but she ignored me. "There is a hammering at the door, and one of them opens it. Maybe Tammy. And the boys come in. Let's say for now it's the Sureños. Maybe he burgled some place for them, or he stole something that belongs to them. Whatever the case, they either want it or they want to know where it is. Okay so far?"

"Keep shingin', shweetheart, you're doing fine."

"So they slap him around a bit. They tie him to the chair, and they lay into him. What's she doing meantime? She's crying, 'Don't hurt him, don't kill him,' yadda yadda. Then what? She's getting on the Sureños' nerves and they shoot her? They threaten him, if he doesn't talk they shoot her? Maybe she tried to protect him. Point is, for some reason they shoot her . . ." She sighed and shook her head. "But it doesn't make any sense. The report says the two shots were close together. So, what, they shot her and then shot him? Why, if they were after information that one of them had? Why kill both? Maybe they got the information and decided to kill them both, but then why take her away with them and leave him?" She stared at me through her aviators. "Shooting her doesn't make sense."

"That's the bit I'm having trouble visualizing."

"So where do we go from here?"

"We need more background. We need to carry out research."

"What kind of research?"

I looked out at the oppressive, sweltering city outside. I turned to her and grinned. "You know? San Francisco rarely rises above sixty-eight Fahrenheit, even at the height of summer."

CHAPTER 3

Back at the station, the air-con still wasn't fixed. Dehan grabbed a bottle of cold water from the dispenser and set herself to doing a background check on Tamara Gunthersen. I went to have a chat with the captain.

He scowled out of the open window from his desk, and the ventilator moved his hair on its steady sweep across the room. He had his jacket slung on the back of his chair, and I could see the damp patches on his shirt under his arms.

"San Francisco, huh? How long for?"

"I wouldn't think more than a day or two at most."

He turned a smile on me that was less a smile than a malevolent leer. "This wouldn't be just an excuse, would it, John? I wouldn't mind a couple of days in the Bay myself—get away from this infernal heat!"

"No, sir, but I do think it is important to get the background on Tamara Gunthersen. At the moment, the whole case seems to revolve around her. It seems Baxter's client is trying to find out what happened to her. Her past may hold the key to what she was doing here, and why they were both killed."

"Hmmm . . . well, if you think it's essential. But just a couple of days, John, and try to keep your expenses down, will you?"

"Of course, sir."

I skipped down the stairs feeling somewhat buoyed and found Dehan at her desk, on the phone. She hung up as I sat down.

"Tamara Gunthersen has no police record. Information available on her—" She tapped at her computer and brought up the research she'd done while I was talking to the captain. "She was a homeowner; property is a house on Brooks Street, San Mateo. There is no foreclosure notice on it, so I'm guessing the mortgage was all paid up. She had a credit card, and she is listed as having defaulted on payments for the last two years. She has a bank account with First Republic that is in credit. That's what I have been able to find out so far."

"Good work."

"I also called the lab and asked them if they had taken samples of the blood on the floor. He wasn't sure, so I asked him to find out. I also asked him, if they *had*, to please analyze it and compare it with Stephen's. And if it wasn't his, to run it through the system."

"Great. Good work." I gazed out the window. The long dusk was settling outside, preparatory to a muggy, sultry evening. "We'll need to look inside her house. I'll get the captain to clear it with the San Mateo PD." I turned to face her. "Book us on the first flight out of here, Dehan. Then let's go pack."

WE TOUCHED down at San Francisco International Airport at eleven a.m. the following morning. The sun was bright, but the temperature was an agreeable sixty-eight degrees. I had rented a Mustang V8 convertible, because I like to have a good car, and we turned left out of the airport along the Bayshore Freeway, with the wind in our hair, and headed for San Mateo.

Dehan had booked us a couple of rooms at the Hillsdale Inn, which was about a mile and a half from Brooks Street, where Tamara had her house. The hotel was remarkable for being completely unremarkable, and also for having a parking lot the size of an international airport. We checked into our rooms, which were functional, and Dehan called Hank, our liaison officer at the San Mateo Police Department, which was two hundred yards away, across East Hillsdale Boulevard.

We met him in the lobby fifteen minutes later. He was big and friendly and looked as though he'd put on his even bigger brother's clothes by mistake that morning. He walked toward us with big strides and shook hands with us like he was really genuinely pleased to meet us. He shoveled his floppy blond hair out of his face and pulled an envelope from a small folder he was carrying.

"I talked to the judge yesterday evening, Dehan, and explained the situation—you were coming from New York, grounds for suspecting homicide, blah blah—and got you a search warrant for the premises. Do you need me to come along?" I drew breath to answer, but he didn't let me. "Strictly, I should, but I am happy to let you go on your own if that works for you. Obviously, if you need to damage the property in any way, dig, knock down walls, blah blah, you should call me. Or if you find anything of importance like a meth lab or a body. But if you are just going to look around . . ." He made a face and spread his hands—hands I figured were pretty full and could do without babysitting visitors from the Big Apple.

"We're fine. We'll call you if anything major shows up."

He handed me a card. "I've arranged for a locksmith to meet you there in . . ." He glanced at his watch. "Twenty minutes. You'll report back to me when you're done?"

We told him we would and made our way to the car as he strode back to his, shoveling his hair out of his face once more.

It was a short drive down East Hillside Boulevard and left onto South Norfolk. Brooks Street was in a quiet, residential area that couldn't have been further from the Bronx. Tamara had a cute, two-story house beyond what had probably been a nice front garden two years ago, with a crazy paved path winding through flower beds to a friendly red door by a big bow window. Today it was overgrown and running to seed.

The locksmith was there, waiting in his van. He unlocked the door for us, made us sign a piece of paper, and went on his way. We stepped inside.

There was a pile of mail behind the door. Dehan hunkered down to gather it up. The place smelled musty and unlived-in. The drapes were drawn, and there was only a filtering of light to alleviate the gloom. To the right of the door, a flight of stairs rose to an upper floor. To the left, there was an open-plan living room, dining area, and a kitchen, separated by a breakfast bar. There was a sofa and two chairs arranged around a TV. A framed photograph of a very pretty young girl with a middle-aged man and woman stood on a small bookcase that held mainly DVDs and CDs. The books were Carlos Castaneda's Don Juan trilogy, three books by Stanislavski, *Norma Jean* by Fred Lawrence Guiles, and three self-help books by authors I had never heard of: *Dream Yourself Happy*, *It's Not Your Fault*, and *Rebirth in Life: A Guide to Rebecoming*. There was also a scrapbook in which she had pasted reviews of plays she had been in.

As I was reading through them, I became aware of the hum of the fridge. There was a table lamp nearby, and I reached out and switched it on. It cast a dull, amber glow. Dehan was at the table leafing through the mail and turned to look at me. I stood, went to the kitchen, and opened the fridge. It was full of rotting, moldy cheese and vegetables. I closed it and leaned on the breakfast bar to look at Dehan.

She said, "There's been enough money in her bank to cover her electricity bills, which must have been minimal. But more important than that, she was intending to come home. She was not planning on staying in New York, or on disappearing. If she had been, she would have cleaned out her account and disconnected the electricity."

I nodded. "What have you got there?"

"Not much. A few bills, invoices. But this could be useful. It seems she's an actress; this is a letter from her agent, Philip Shaw."

I frowned. "I didn't think anybody wrote letters anymore."

"These are statements. Maybe she wanted hard copies." She glanced at me and smiled. "Maybe her agent is a dinosaur."

"There are a few of us left. We'd better go and have a talk with him."

We had a look upstairs. There were still clothes in her closet and her dresser. They were of a surprising variety, from torn jeans and sweatshirts to elegant ball gowns and cocktail dresses, from the demure to the downright outrageous. Dehan raised an eyebrow at them. "I guess an actress needs all this."

"Most women," I said, with the air of one who knew, "like to dress differently for different occasions. They don't wear the same jeans and boots day in, day out."

"Like you'd know."

She had a dressing table with lots of makeup, and in the bathroom, her toothbrush was gone, but most of her toiletries were still there. Dehan sat on the end of the bed and scrunched up her face.

"So here is an actress, living in a nice house in the Bay Area. She has an agent, and she is obviously working because she has money in the bank and she's keeping this house on her own. One day she ups and goes to New York, but not just New York—the Bronx. She is not planning to stay there; she is planning to come back soon, so it's just a visit. While she's there, she visits this loser, Stephen Springfellow, the Sureños show up, beat seven bales of shit out of him, and then shoot them both. They leave him dead where he is on the chair, and take her body away with them."

I was leaning on the bathroom doorjamb listening to her. "Doesn't make a lot of sense. We need to know why she went to New York."

"Maybe she got a gig there and that's how she met Stephen . . ." But even as she said it, she was looking unconvinced. "He doesn't strike me as the theatergoing type. I think they met here."

There was something nagging at the back of my mind. "Didn't the file say Stephen had been living in San Francisco?"

She nodded. "Yeah, for a couple of years. Then went back east in 2014. They could have met here."

"So maybe she went back for some kind of reconciliation."

"Why suddenly? What happened to make her suddenly want to go out east and meet up with him?"

"We need to talk to her agent."

Scan the QR code below to purchase LET US PREY.
Or go to: righthouse.com/let-us-prey

Made in the USA
Las Vegas, NV
01 March 2025

18905659R00125